REFORMATION - PART 1

Book one in the Psychic Knights series

BY

P.B.THOMPSON

Copyright © 2011 P.B.THOMPSON
Published by FERRET PUBLISHING LTD

All rights reserved.
This is a work of fiction. Names, characters, places and incidents are products of the author's imagination or are used fictitiously. Any similarity to actual persons, organisations, and/or events is purely coincidental.

ISBN: 1514650762
ISBN-13: 978-1514650769

Cover image from:
http://www.123rf.com/profile_spinningangel

OTHER NOVELS BY P.B.THOMPSON

Psychic Knights Series:
Reformation - Part 1
Reformation - Part 2
Reformation - Part 3
Destiny
Revenge
The Needle of Chorlook
Wormhole

The Trygor Legends Series:
The Staff of Xandra
Forests of Koreen
Portuse Caves

The Nobody Man Series:
Not My Mind

The Assassins of Fortune Series:
Island of the Hunted

Crime:
Deadly Decisions

SHORT STORIES BY P.B.THOMPSON

The Psychic Knights World:
Down Comes the Night
The Cavalry Cometh
Feeling Alive
Sweet Lady
Crash Landing
Rat King
Ryony
Strine City Stand Off
Darkness Descends
Parameen Rescue
Psychic Knights Adventures - Anthology

Crime:
A Crime Triple

Horror:
Horror Duet 1 (Terror Tales)
Horror Duet 2 (Terror Tales)
Horror Duet 3 (Terror Tales)
Terror Tales Collection

P.B.THOMPSON LINKS

For free excerpts of other P.B.Thompson books go to:
http://pbthompson.wordpress.com/

and find out about future projects at
http://www.ferretpublishing.com/

To join the mailing list for future release dates please email:
pbthompson@zoho.com

CHAPTER ONE

Now

He struggled to open his eyes. Fighting with consciousness, the bright surroundings forced him to squint as his eyelids slowly lifted. He tried to move his arms, but found they were restrained. No, not restrained. Just immobile. The same for his legs. He felt no pain. Just an inability to move.

Still fighting to stay conscious, his eyes finally focused on what was above him. A smooth, white ceiling. No markings. Just an ocean of white that for all he knew went on forever. He managed to move his head slightly. Softness could be felt. At least he had some feeling.

Lavender! He could smell smoky lavender filling his nostrils as his head turned. His eyes saw movement. Coming towards him.

"Thorn, you're..."

Panic set in. He tried to move again, but couldn't and his head started swimming until he lost consciousness again.

***

Nine days earlier

The inconspicuous world lay in a Solar System many light years from Earth. It was one of three habitable planets that orbited the white sun. Prius 3 was mostly barren. A chunk of rock floating around the sun with no signs of life except the thick vegetation that covered a quarter of the planet. A perfect hiding place.

Within naturally formed caves and valleys a community had formed over the last hundred years. These innocent humans had been hunted and hounded away from their home planet by the TechPsychers. These were the lucky ones. They had been saved by the small rebel groups that had grown from the persecution. Others had been captured and taken away to unknown destinations. All because of their natural abilities.

High up in one of the caverns that overlooked a green valley a craft was coming into land. Its flashing landing lights illuminating part of the cavern. When it landed it coasted to the nearest docking point and the hatchway opened to let out fifty passengers. All a little shaken and tired from their recent ordeal. A greeting party came to meet them and ushered them to the back of the cavern where they were taken in lifts to the waiting medical staff.

On the craft the five man strong crew were making their weapons safe and running checks on the craft itself.

"Akarn, go and get that arm seen to. We'll take care of the equipment."

"OK, but don't start the celebrating until I get back.

I've still got another good arm to hold my glass with."

The five men grinned in unison as though they were in a synchronised grinning competition. "Don't worry big man. We'll wait for you."

Akarn heaved his massive bulk out of the ship and headed for the infirmary keeping hold of his injured arm. He was at least a foot taller than the rest of the group and almost twice as wide, most of his bulk being muscle. His skin was as dark as coal and the only blemeshes were the scars from previous injuries.

"Another successful mission," said Ifor stretching out his legs after the long trip back. "Those TechPsychers are so dumb. The vegetation outside put up more resistance when we were clearing it than they did." Ifor was checking his Vibro-Gun; his favoured weapon. He was six foot two inches tall and solidly built with receding hair that had been saying goodbye to his head since he was in his thirties. His light brown skinned face was hard and he had a look that could win a fight even before a fist was raised.

"Don't get too carried away. You know they're never always that easy. We still need to make sure we are well prepared for the next time." The cautionary tone came from Thorn.

"Ah! Come on Thorn. The TechPsychers are pussies. We're just too good for them and our record speaks for itself." Yilnar slid back on the bench he was on and rested against the bulkhead. "How long have we been together? Seventy, eighty years. How many people have we rescued? Thousands! And how many fatal casualties have we suffered? None! None of the other groups can match us and neither can the TechPsychers."

"We owe a lot to intelligence and planning. Don't

forget that."

"Who does the planning? We do," Ifor said.

Thorn smiled. His chiselled features softened as his teeth showed. He too was six foot two inches tall with a slender, but strong build that had formed over the many years he had trained for the numerous combat situations he and his team had been exposed to. His once full head of hair had been shaved almost bald and the sweat glistened on his pale skin.

"OK, so we are good. But don't let it go to your heads."

Ifor and Yilnar let out a cheer just as Roman walked in from the engine compartment.

"How is she?" Thorn had to shout to be heard.

"A little TLC and she'll be fine. What's going on?" Roman looked over at the two men cheering.

"We're just getting in the celebratory mood," Ifor said.

"Well boys, let's get packed up and start that celebrating. I've got to go and see the old man first. I'll meet you in the Valley bar as soon as I've finished." Thorn slung his back pack over his shoulder and collected up his weapons. "And order some of those Chilli Chicken Wraps. I'm starving."

***

Now

Once again Thorn wrestled with his consciousness trying to stay alert. The white ceiling came into focus again. He turned his head to a sound. A clunking mechanical sound. He could make out two humanoid figures. Mechanical figures working at what looked like a wall of computers at the far end of the room. Flashing lights played on his eyes sending a stabbing pain to his brain. He shut his eyes tight shielding them from the source of the pain. His mind began to swim again. No! He fought to stay awake, but slipped into unconsciousness once more.

CHAPTER TWO

Nine Days Earlier

Thorn returned his weapons to stock. Although, officially the weapons were shared amongst the teams in the encampment, in reality each member of Thorn's team had their own selection. Their own personal favourites that had been modified to their own preferences. And Gillon, the stock supervisor was the one who made the modifications.

"Another successful trip, Thorn? There are already stories of how you and your team took out a whole detail of TechPsychers. Eight ships was the last count I heard." Gillon took the stubby Vibro-Gun and Laser Pistol, Thorn's personal choice, and stacked them in the rack reserved for the Psychic Knights. Thorn gave a sly grin.

"Typical gossip. It was only five ships. Take a look at the Vibro-Gun for me. It seems to be lacking in power." He turned away.

"Will do. Good to have you back."

The old man, Tor-Pic, had an office two hundred metres below the landing bay overlooking the lush valley. Cut from the rock, it was sparsely furnished. Just a chair and the Holo-Computer that kept track of all of his teams and intelligence agents spread throughout the galaxy. The Holo-Computer, set into the floor, projected numerous displays upwards filling the space between the chair and the view out into the valley. Though Tor-Pic controlled the Holo-Computer with his mind, he preferred to view the data on screen. At two hundred and ninety and on his third and final regeneration he liked to keep his physical body in good working order.

His white hair barely covered his oversized cranium. The dark eyebrows were the only remnants of the colour his hair once was. A sullen look permanently etched on his face was the result of the fight with the TechPsychers over the last hundred years. He wore dark leather trousers and a dark leather waistcoat over a white collarless shirt.

'Are you free to see me now?'

The request came through to Tor-Pic's mind.

'Of course! Come in my boy,' he replied.

Thorn entered the room with a big smile on his face. Tor-Pic greeted his friend as his chair elevated him upright. They both embraced for a few seconds.

"It's good to see you back. And another successful rescue. Fifty more persecuted souls delivered from those damn TechPsychers. You played it to perfection, my boy. As always. Would you like a drink?" He made his way to a unit that was set in to the far wall.

"Sure, why not?"

"Your usual?"

Thorn gave a casual nod. Tor-Pic projected his order

to the machine and two glasses materialised in the opening at the bottom filled with ice cubes and shots of Earth rum. Both men gave a quick salute with the glasses and downed the drink in one.

Thorn nodded to the displays around the room.

"How are the other teams doing?"

Tor-Pic walked towards them. "We lost half of Borren's team on ReesEr 9," he said pointing to one display. "Unfortunately the rescue failed." He paused for a short moment. "We've had two other successes, saving a total of fourteen people." Tor-Pic looked at Thorn. The total helplessness he felt could be seen on his face. "We're not getting many intelligence reports through. The opportunities for rescues are few and far between. The rest of the teams are still here on base." He turned back to the displays. "We may have one coming through soon. A big one, but I've had false hope about these before so I'm not getting too excited."

"Any more news on why the TechPsychers are doing this?"

Tor-Pic shook his head. He went back to the dispenser and requested another two drinks.

"Other than the theory that they feel threatened by us, no. We haven't got the resources to track them once their ships go into Hyperspace with our people on them. I find it hard to believe that they would transport them somewhere just to kill them. They must be using them for something. But until we have more bodies out in the field all we can do is rescue the ones we know about and hope we come across something that can end this nightmare."

"We will, and make them pay for all the suffering they have caused. We have to believe we will find a weakness in their technology and bring them down." Thorn finished his second drink.

"I've got two hundred people searching the entire galaxy. Half of them looking for our people and the other half keeping us up to date with the TechPsychers movements. Nowhere nearly enough. It's getting harder and harder to keep that belief." Tor-Pic gulped down the rest of his drink. "Enough of this defeatism. You must be eager to get back to your men to celebrate this latest victory. You head off there and I'll pass by a little later to join you."

They both embraced again and Thorn left.

CHAPTER THREE

Distant laser shots gently woke Thorn. He probed the room with his mind until he found the clock. Nine thirty. A full eight hours sleep. 'I haven't done that in a while,' he thought. 'Mind you, the drinking session with the boys must have helped.' More laser fire. 'The idle teams must be getting some combat training in.'

The white sun shone through the cracks in the shutters of the hut leaving bright stripes on his bed. The dust in the air glittered as it danced around him.

Pulling back the cover he got out of bed scratching the back of his head. As he stepped down he felt the throb from an old wound. Walking to the fridge with a slight limp he got out a bottle of water. More laser fire fizzed outside as he took a swig from the bottle. Then an explosion. 'Jees! Have they used enough explosives?' The sarcastic thought disappeared as soon as he felt a gentle nudge on his mind. Someone wanted to psych talk with him. He opened up.

'Thorn, it's Tor. I've had some interesting feedback

from one of our men on Earth. Come and see me when you've got a minute. I'll be in the Strategy Room.'
'OK, I'll just get something to eat and I'll come by.'

The early sun shone brightly behind the tall rocks casting long shadows over the Porta-Habs. The area below the caves in the valley had been cleared and Porta-Habs erected for the serving Team members. Further down the valley were the civilians that had been rescued and decided to stay on Prius 3. Most of the rescued were relocated on other worlds, but a small community had stayed, which numbered in the thousands. They stayed to help with the on-going struggle against the TechPsychers. Technicians, medical staff, teachers for the kids, and the usual bars and gambling places that had grown for the basics of human needs.

He made the short walk to the mess hall taking in his favourite views of the sloping valley that led down into the built up living area and onto the lush vegetation. As he opened the door he was greeted with a short cheer.

"You finally got out of your stinking pit, then," Ifor said. The rest of the Psychic Knights were there already.

Thorn smiled and said, "I don't know about you guys, but I sure needed that sleep". He grabbed a plate and began filling it up from the selection of food that had been laid out. It was so nice to have proper food again.

"We were just having a little chat about what we're going to do next. Seeing as there doesn't seem to be anything lined up for us and as there are so many teams here still, maybe we could have a short break for a week or so. We've been out in the field for the last month. I think we deserve a rest. We were just discussing about going to Nexuss. The planet's well known for its pleasure arcades and gambling halls. At least in the southern hemisphere." Yilnar looked around the room as everyone nodded in agreement. His lineage hailed from the Mediterranean and his dusky tan seemed to accentuate his pearl white teeth and shocking black hair. Two inches shorter than Thorn and Ifor, his broad shoulders and thick set, muscular body made him a more imposing figure.

"Want to throw away your credits, eh? Didn't you learn anything from last night down in the valley?"

"Yeah, he learnt that not everyone wearing a dress is a woman." Everyone burst out laughing at Akarn's rare quip.

"You may have to put that on hold. I've just been summoned by the old man. He may have something for us yet," Thorn managed to get out through his laughing.

"Well if there's anything I like more than gambling it's breaking a few of them TechPsychers heads." Akarn ground his massive fist into his palm. "Any idea where we're off to?"

"Nope. Not yet. As soon as I've eaten I'm going to see him, now budge over and let me fill my empty belly."

An hour later Thorn was standing in the Strategy Room pouring over data on the displays in front of Tor-Pic's chair. A detailed map was shown on one of them. An aerial view of the same area was displayed on another. A cluster of buildings could be seen within a clearing that had been roughly gouged out from a jungle area on Earth. No rescue attempts had ever been made on Earth before. The departure areas that held the captives before they were taken off world were too heavily guarded, even for Thorn's team.

"This is the best chance we've ever had of making a rescue on Earth. And it will be the biggest rescue attempt we've ever tried. Up to three hundred captives are in this area. You've got the best team for the job, Thorn." Tor-Pic pointed to the aerial view and singled out one of the buildings. "They're held in this building. We're not too sure why they are there. Our sources think it may be some sort of experimentation area. Away from the public eye. Whatever it is the same objectives apply. Rescue the captives and come away with no casualties."

Thorn looked concerned. "We've never attempted anything on Earth before because it's too risky. What makes you so sure this is any safer?"

Tor-Pic glared at him. "Our sources are reliable. This is one of the best opportunities to save a lot of our people. We have all the information we need for getting on and off the planet without being detected. We have men on the inside that can disable the areas network of scanners for the time that it will take for you to set down. Every last detail has been taken care of."

A frown crept over Thorn's face. "Could our source have been compromised?"

The old man shook his head. "Impossible! All the checks we have in place confirm our cover is still secure." He grabbed Thorn's arm firmly and stared at him with an intensity that burned deep in Thorn's soul. His voice lowered. "A rescue of this scale is very rare. Who knows what's going on down there! We have to save these people!"

Thorn hesitated. The old man was getting emotional. He hadn't seen him like this before and he wondered if his emotions were affecting his decisions. Finally he answered.

"It goes against my better judgement, but we'll do it. I'll confer with the men and we'll come up with a plan."

"We have a time scale for this one. Our source can disable the scanning network at 0700 hours Earth time five days from now for five minutes. And then again 0700 hours two days later for when the rescue is complete."

Thorn's eyes widened when he heard this.

"That's way too soon. It'll take us four days to get there, as long as we have no problems on the way, and it'll be a day for us to get things ready here. I don't like this Tor. This isn't how we've survived all of this time."

"It will be fine, Thorn. You can do your planning on the way and with enough bodies involved we can get you going in half a day."

The emotion in Tor-Pic's voice was prominent now and this new experience took Thorn by surprise. In the eighty or so years he had known Tor-Pic, he was always professional. Thorn reacted as he felt the anger welling up inside.

"Right then, I'll send you a list of the equipment we will need and you get them all put on our ship as soon as you can. In the meantime I'll go over all of the data you have with my men and we'll see if we can come up with something that will help us survive this fiasco." He turned and stormed out of the room.

CHAPTER FOUR

Now

Again the white ceiling came into view as Thorn's consciousness returned. His head pounded like a disciples praying drum. The smell of lavender once again tickled his senses.

"He's coming around again," he heard close by.

Slowly turning his head his vision focussed on the figure that stood next to him; the source of the voice. A bipedal figure that could have passed for a naked human body apart from the lack of genitals and extra pair of arms. On closer inspection the skin looked unnatural as though it had been manufactured. On the shoulders sat an unusually long, slender neck attached to a humanoid head. Blue in colour with smooth velvety, hairless skin. The black eyes sat deep in their sockets and the lipless mouth formed into what looked like a smile. The face had no nose, but on the side of the long neck there was a series of slits like fish gills. Two dish-like objects protruded from the side of the head that seemed to be made of the same material as the body.

"Can you hear me Thorn?"

"Who...are...you? Where...am...I?"

"You've come round too soon. Your mind has been through a serious trauma. You need more time. Can you remember anything? Who you are?"

Thorn shook his head slowly.

"I am Torst. You are on a planet called Riigel. I picked you up from your Home world, called Earth." Torst looked up at a monitoring machine above where Thorn lay. "He's going again." A second alien came over to join him looking identical in almost every way to Torst save a few minor differences in the features on his blue face. "I've never seen anything like it before. His brain is repairing itself at a phenomenal rate."

Thorn closed his eyes as the blackness enveloped him again.

***

Four Days Earlier

The Psychic Knights ship and the accompanying transporter made it safely onto Earth in the time frame they had. Exactly as planned. To the point where Thorn thought it was too easy.

Both ships had landed in a small clearing five miles to the east of the target area. Roman had deployed his scouting droids, small spherical objects that glided through the air as quiet as a whisper. They mapped the area with finite accuracy. Avoiding and marking any detection grids and plotting the best path to the intended target. Any one of the Psychic Knights could see through and control the droids with their minds, but the initial scout was unaided.

Some of the team were going through their equipment once more when the droids returned. The data was already in the ships computer and Roman sifted through it with computer like speed. He was a scrawny man compared to the others, though as fit as any of them. His styled afro hair sat on his head like a perfectly fitting hat. The boyish features of his face hid the one hundred year old man inside, although he was still only in his first regeneration. His skill was with machines. He had a small collection that he took on every mission. Though he was proficient with weapons and unarmed combat, his forte was the use of his little army. His mind wasn't strong enough to control anything bigger than the size of a small dog, but his creations were the first line of attack, and in some cases won the battle for them.

'How's it looking, Roman?' Thorn had to psychically communicate with Roman as his mind was locked into the computer.

'I'll be done in about ten minutes.'

'OK. There'll be some food waiting for you outside when you're finished.'

Outside the rest of the team were finishing up with their equipment and chatting with the crew of the transporter. Although their ship, the Savage Mind, was a good size, it could hold only eighty plus crew. The transporter and its crew had been on missions with the Psychic Knights before and they knew each other well. The captain, Dar-Fur, was once an active member of a rescue team until most of them got wiped out during a mission and he sustained a long-term injury. As well as being a tough fighter out in the field he was a skilled pilot and after sustaining the injury signed up for piloting transporters. Now three hundred and seven, he had used the third and last of his regenerations.

He scratched the side of his head, displacing a bunch of his long grey hair. His wrinkled features creased even more as he took Ifor's recent jibe in the manner it was given.

"You'll be lucky to live as long as me let alone become as good looking as me."

A roar of laughter came from the group of seven. Thorn joined them from the ship.

"Glad to see you are all in good spirits. Let's hope we'll be in the same mood in two day's time."

"You're still not convinced about this one then, Thorn?" Dar-Fur stood up and collected some food from the table that had been set-up as he asked the question. He seemed to drag his mechanical leg as he walked. He'd never gotten used to it in all the time he'd had it.

"I just want everyone to be a bit more cautious when we make our move. It all seems too...simple."

"The best plans usually are," this from one of Dar-Fur's crew.

"One of the reasons we've survived this long is that we've made our own plans from information provided. To our own time-scales. Most of that has been taken out of our hands this time."

Dar-Fur swallowed his food before speaking.

"The old man seems pretty certain the information is OK. Looks like you're gonna have to rely on someone else this time. He really wants this one. It'll be the biggest rescue we've ever made and I get the feeling he thinks it could lead to a few more on this planet."

"That's one of my worries. He seems to be making decisions based on emotions. That's not how you should prepare for these rescues."

Roman came down the Savage Minds ramp.

"All done. Some interesting detection systems out there, but they won't pose much of a problem for my babies when the time comes. Now where's that food?" He headed over to the table.

It was now late morning and the sun was high in the sky. The heat was uncomfortable in direct sunlight due to the poor ozone cover, but Dar-Fur and some of his crew had erected a solar shade, which also provided an air-conditioned area for the group to shelter in.

"Have you outlined the danger areas yet?" Thorn took a swig from his container of water.

"All in the ships computer."

"OK. Have you sent the droids out to set-up a perimeter of a thousand metres yet? I don't want any surprises."

"It was the first thing I did when we landed. As I always do. You know that." Roman got a little annoyed at Thorn's questions. He'd never needed to be reminded of his responsibilities before.

Thorn walked towards the ship.

"I'll be inside going over the plans again."

Ifor sensed Roman's change in mood.

"Don't take it to heart. He's a bit more on edge than usual. We all are. We're going out on a limb on this one and relying on people outside of our group more than we'd like to."

"Maybe, but he knows us. He knows we're as careful and cautious as he is." Roman collected his food and sat down. The tension in the air had risen and the light hearted banter had ceased.

Suddenly the detection warning signal made Thorn's

men jump to attention. The signal was tuned to their minds so none of the transporter crew knew what was going on. Thorn came to the top of the ramp.

"We've got a flyer coming in overhead!"

"Have they detected us?" Ifor questioned.

"No. The cloaking device is doing its job, but I want everyone armed and ready. We all know what happened on Serina."

The four of them dropped everything and armed themselves.

"What happened on Serina?" Dar-Fur asked Yilnar.

"A flyer nearly landed on top of us. The cloaking device works so well masking the ship and any noises coming from it that it's as if there is a clear landing area where we are. The trouble with Serina was we camped on what was a local hunting area and there was a party looking forward to a day's hunting. The pilot must have nearly had a heart attack when his proximity alarms went off."

The noise of the flyer was now audible to everyone. Coming from the east it cruised just above the tree tops making them sway in the back wash. The shrill of the engines scattered the local wildlife. Both crews on the ground had retreated to the safety of their cloaked ships. Thorn and Roman both watched its progress on the Holo-Screen. As it flew almost directly over them Ifor gently squeezed on his Vibro-Cannon. The sound of the engines above started to recede.

"Any more coming in?" asked Akarn.

"Nope. That's the only one," replied Roman.

"OK, panic over." Thorn went back to his plans and the others returned to the solar shade.

"What do you think that was?" Dar-Fur asked from

the doorway of his ship as he saw Roman coming out of the Savage Mind.

"Just a transporter," said Roman.

"Carrying more prisoners?"

Roman glanced back at Ifor before replying,

"Possibly. Or it could just be supplies. There's no way of knowing."

"Let's hope it is supplies. We only have enough room left for a handful of people." The group returned to their seats and gradually eased back in to the light-hearted conversation from earlier until just after midday when they filtered back to their respective ships.

The rest of the day was spent checking arms and going over the plans for the rescue. Each member of the Psychic Knights digested the target area information and gave input on how to improve the chances of success. A ritual that they went through before every mission.

The sun began to set casting long shadows from the trees surrounding the camp. After finalising the rescue plans, Ifor and Akarn sat outside with three of the transporter crew discussing previous missions they had been on. Ifor had finished regaling everyone with the story of their last mission when Chero-Deen, a young woman in her forties, spoke.

"Is it true you can lift a transporter with your mind?" Her question was so soft Ifor could just about hear her. He gave a hearty laugh.

"Where did you hear that?" he asked.

"I heard it first in class and it's also been repeated in taverns and eateries back on Prius 3. They say that every one of you can stop a transporter in flight and when you join your minds together you are strong enough to move a moon."

Both Ifor and Akarn looked at each other and burst out laughing. It was a full minute before Ifor could answer. He wiped the tears from his eyes.

"My, how our reputations have grown. Even if they are borne from fantasy. No, we cannot move transporters with our minds, and as for moving moons," he gave a little chuckle. "I dread to think how that came about. We can only move small objects, just like yourself and everyone on Prius 3. We can influence people with our minds a lot more than most and create a small field to defend ourselves and our communication with each other is a lot more advanced than anyone else, but other than that we are just like you."

Both men could see the disappointment in the young woman's eyes. A myth destroyed in an instant. Ifor tried to recover some sort of mythical status for the girl.

"What we lack in your expectations we more than make up for in bravery. You will see the day after tomorrow when we fight. There isn't a man or woman that can match us."

The girl gave a weak smile.

The night brought a clear cold sky and with it the night time chorus of the living jungle. Stars blinked overhead as if trying to send a message in code, but the darkness absorbed their light, offering no reply. Thorn had a restless night until finally he gave up trying to sleep and went back over the rescue plans once again.

CHAPTER FIVE

Early the next morning Roman's droids were out scouting once again. This time with Roman, Yilnar and Akarn all taking a first-hand look by setting their minds in the droids. The distance the droids travelled was too far for the men to take full control, but they could experience the area by allowing their minds to become passive passengers within the droids. They got a feel for the area by experiencing the physical locations rather than relying on the viewing of three dimensional maps. The heavy undergrowth and dense population of trees clearly visible through the Optically Readjusted Vision mode of the droids and the enhanced sensors provided real-time feel for the rest of their senses.

"Where's Thorn?" Roman asked the group sat outside having breakfast.

"He went for a walk. It looked like he didn't have a good night's sleep." The reply came from Brahman, the transporters Medic. He had just sat down with his food as Roman came down the ramp.

'Thorn, are you there?' he sent. A few seconds went by.

'What is it?'

'We've had a communication from our agent inside. He needs to speak to you. He said he'll try again at 11:30am.'

'OK. I'll be back by then.'

The path of communication went dead as Thorn broke off. Roman returned to the command deck where Ifor was playing cards with Akarn.

"Did you find him?" Ifor asked.

"No, but I psyched him. I think he's out there practising again. I could feel the strain on his mind when I linked up."

Ifor shook his head.

"It's the wrong time to be doing that sort of thing. He needs to be in top shape for when we make our move later. Apart from the fact he's wasting his time. How long has he been trying to strengthen his mind? Too long. I've told him time and time again there's only one way to do that and it's through surgery and I only know of two people who survived going under the laser. And they only lasted two months afterwards. It's about time he gave up."

Akarn showed his cards and grinned.

"Can you beat that?"

Ifor looked at them and growled with annoyance. He threw his cards down and the big man collected his winnings.

"I love playing with you," Akarn said. "You love to donate your credits so easily." The smile on his face almost reached his ears.

"Just deal the next hand and don't take them credits anywhere. They're coming straight back."

The clearing that Thorn had found was just a twenty minute walk from the landing site. An area of flattened vegetation, it was about a hundred square metres in size. Ever since he had control over what his mind could do, something deep inside made him feel as though this was just the tip of what he was capable of. There were stories of individuals, somewhere in the galaxy in travelling circuses that could pull trees out of the ground or lift small Land Cruisers in the air with just their mind. Although no documented proof of these people existed the stories still persisted. He didn't know what he could be capable of, but he felt there was something more that was possible. Something, maybe, that no one else had ever done.

And yet, no matter how often he practised he had made very little progress. Whenever he found time he could spend alone he would concentrate hard. Searching within his mind for that elusive key to unlock the limits that were forced upon him by nature.

The tree branch crashed to the floor once again as it slipped from his minds grasp like a toy from a child's hand that was too heavy. If he was one of the others, he would have given up long ago. None of them believed the mind could do more and none of them tried.

He sat down on a fallen tree trunk, dejected, but not beaten. He noticed an ant at his foot. In its grasp a leaf that was five times the size of its body. He saw it drop the leaf, then dance around a little and pick it back up, walk on a few more paces then drop it again. This cycle continued until it was gone. How determination and belief could overcome the hardest of obstacles no matter how small you were. A lesson Thorn kept in his mind as he stood up and tried again.

Later that morning Thorn was back in the Savage Mind waiting for contact from their inside man; something else that had never had to happen before.

It was coming up to 11:50am and the discomfort of the situation was beginning to gnaw at his mind until a beep from the comms speaker interrupted his train of thought. He saw it was coming in on an encrypted channel with the correct code and answered.

"Speak to me." There was a moment's pause.

"Thorn, it is an honour to finally speak to you. You and your teams exploits give us all hope that one day we will be able to live freely."

Thorn was in no mood for a long conversation.

"Thank you. Now what seems to be the problem."

"The prisoners are to be moved tonight. This has meant an increase in security personnel."

"By how many?"

"By another sixty guards. They were brought in yesterday. I only found out about the move this morning."

"Damn! I knew there was going to be problems."

"From what I hear about your team another sixty personnel shouldn't be a problem."

Thorn sneered.

"It's not the amount, it's the fact that an unexpected event has happened."

The voice on the other end spoke quite casually. "Unfortunately these things happen."

This flippant remark got Thorn's back up and he gave

a stinging reply.

"When we plan missions these unexpected events are never unexpected." There was a pause. "Does this affect our timings?"

"No. Everything is as planned," came back a timid voice. "The defence system will come down at 1700 hours for planned maintenance for 10 minutes. Giving you enough time to get in undetected. During this time the patrols will increase, but you've taken this into account. The additional personnel are stationed in the far building at the West side of the complex well away from the prisoners. All that's left is for me to wish you well."

Thorn mellowed a little after the last remark. He could feel the sincerity in the voice.

"Thanks. Are you sure you won't come back with us?"

"No, I can still do more good here. My tracks are covered so I will be safe."

"Until 1700 hours then." Thorn ended the comms link. He turned to his men.

"Looks like we have a little extra company."

"We'll need a few more droids then," Roman said. "I'd better start prepping them now." With that he jumped up and left.

A grin spread across Ifor's face.

"I thought they were making it too easy for us. Now at least there's a bit of a challenge."

"Well we'd better revise our plan of attack a little bit to account for the extra guards. We'll meet on the Obs deck in, say, thirty minutes. That should give Roman enough time."

An hour later and the five men began their own personal preparations. With the revised plans made, departure time was in less than an hour. Each mission afforded its own preparation time. Some longer than others, but always enough time to go through each man's rituals. Some just going through a walk-through in their minds of what was going to happen, others saying a small prayer or kissing the photo of their long departed families. Whichever one it was, it was done in their own personal space, away from the others.

CHAPTER SIX

At 1400 hours the sun shone down in a clear blue sky. The heat had opened the Prearus flower, a native of Prearus 6 in the Delta Sector which had been brought to Earth as a seed by an unsuspecting craft. The sweet aroma hung heavy in the air and attracted the local insects in its quest to spread its seed and begin its domination of yet another planet.

The Magno-Bikes silently left the landing site leaving the Savage Mind and transporter behind. Dar-Fur and his crew waited back in their ship for the signal that the captives were ready to be picked up. The Bikes travelled in single file, droids ahead and behind masking their approach from the light tracking systems that were installed three miles from the complex.

The route planned through the bushes and trees was taken at a steady pace. A route that was marked the day before by one of the droids. When they reached to within a mile of the complex they split up. Each taking four droids until they had the complex surrounded. They stopped in their positions and got off the Bikes.

From this point the tracking systems were a lot more sophisticated. Holo-Pressure pads, infra-red sensing fields, magno-sensing equipment that detected magnetic displacements from the ground to two hundred feet in the air above the tree line.

'Everyone settled?' sent Thorn as he sat on a tree stump. Four confirmations were sent simultaneously.

'OK. Do what you can with the droids. The less guards conscious the easier it will be later on. We have thirty minutes. And remember, the extra guards should be coming on patrol now ready for the system shut-down.'

The Psychic Knights sent their droids off towards the complex, keeping one back as a guard. Each of the men could see through all four of them simultaneously while they were under their control. This gave their initial approach invisibility. The special alloy that Roman had built them from could only be found on Creeshan; a planet that sat at the very edge of the galaxy. This alloy was virtually undetectable by known technology.

Ifor's three droids came across the first guard about five hundred meters from the complex. They hovered fifteen metres above the ground in the cover of the trees canopy as silent as a light summer breeze. Ifor zoomed in on the guard to see what he was doing. He screwed his face up as he saw the guard urinate against a tree.

"Not something I want to be seeing," he muttered to himself.

As soon as the guard had finished and turned to go, he fell to the ground from a burst of sonic energy from the droid that left him unconscious. The second droid quickly activated a light displacement field around the guard making him invisible.

"One down," Ifor said.

Roman's droids were coming up to their first guards. Three of them stood around talking in a small clearing. One of the guards was lighting three Marijuana roll ups. Not your average Marijuana roll ups. The plants that were grown were genetically altered which had side effects when inhaled of enhanced aggression and stamina as well as a high tolerance of pain.

The guard handed round the lighted sticks and each man inhaled as though it was a cool drink on a hot day. One of them began to speak. On his third word he dropped to his knees and then slumped forward. Simultaneously the other two did the same as the three droids sonic energy bursts reached their bodies. The three men ended up as a pile in the thick vegetation covering the floor.

"Damn! Almost got them leaning against each other," Roman said. The droids covered the men with the LDF and continued on cautiously.

Five minutes before the defences came down and the fifteen droids were making good progress. Twenty five men had been neutralised and they were within a hundred metres of the complex perimeter. No physical barrier to the complex existed. No concrete, steel or polymer plastic walls. The buildings inside could be clearly seen. A sparse looking place. Just a large dome building in the centre with five various sized living modules surrounding it. To the south of the site was the landing area for the transport craft.

What did protect these buildings was a deadly, invisible laser field that, as far as the droids could determine on their previous scouting mission, stretched to a height of three hundred metres and domed over the complex. Every fifty metres around the perimeter a laser cannon perched on its platform controlled by the central computer, a synthetic brain. One of a network of organs across Earth feeding information back to the C.O.C at the heart of the TechPsychers Empire.

A door sized hole opened in the laser field, activated by the chip lasered into the first guard's wrist, and eight guards went through. Their grey body suits, made from a synthetic material that kept them cool and gave them some laser fire protection, shimmered in the weakening sunlight. Across their heads a metal band sat secured to neural connectors surgically implanted in their temples. This was what gave the TechPsychers their powers.

Just over a hundred and fifty years ago a mining company acquired alien technology that gave the wearer the ability to control things with their mind. Not like the natural psychers. This was more powerful. Not only could they control things, but they could control people and move objects the size of humans. This gave the mining company, particularly a man called Conrad Preest, the owner, immense power. Within the space of just twenty years an army of TechPsychers, controlled by Preest, had emerged and taken control of Earth and then within another thirty years all sixteen sectors of the galaxy had at least some partial influence from the TechPsychers.

The natural psychers were immune to the mind control and so became hunted, incarcerated and taken to unknown locations off world. The fight for freedom had begun ten years into the TechPsychers domination of Earth. A fight that had led the Psychic Knights to this point in their lives.

A whining noise could be heard from where the men were sitting. The defences were down.

'Let's go!'

The five men jumped on their Magno-Bikes and sped off through the trees. With autopilot engaged in stealth mode the Psychic Knights were free to control their droids.

CHAPTER SEVEN

The guards were now fully deployed in ten groups of eight around the complex sweeping their way outwards from the perimeter. Each group couldn't see the others, but kept in contact psychically.

'Another exciting day out here in the middle of nowhere, Jezza. I'm looking forward to getting back to that pleasure world. The sooner we get rid of these Naturals the better.'

Jezza was the team leader of Gamma team and sat on a tree stump while his men carried out their checks up ahead.

'Are you sure you wanna be going back to that place. They didn't take too kindly to your last visit.'

Drake cast his mind back six months. Their last break from duty. In one of the clubs he was accosted by a dancing girl, though she swore blind that he tripped her in such a way that her naked breasts smothered his face as she fell forward.

'I'm sure they won't remember me. Anyway there are

plenty of other places to go.'

There was a silence from both parties as Ifor's and Thorn's droids took them out simultaneously.

'Impeccable timing as always, Ifor.'
'Likewise, Thorn.'

Both men afforded themselves a smile as their bikes silently carried them towards their goal.

Yilnar was making slower progress due to the heavy vegetation, but was none the less dispatching the guards with deadly accuracy. His droids had rendered four more guards unconscious while he was still three quarters of a mile away. A distance just on the limits of his control.

Roman was having even better success. Fifteen men down and still not spotted. His range of control was greater than the others. He felt this was due to the amount of time he spent fine tuning each droid. Getting to know their souls, for that's what he believed they had. Every droid, every machine had its own personality. Something that, if you spent enough time on, could be tapped into. The others couldn't see this. They just used the droids when they needed them. They couldn't see how bonding with them could be beneficial.

The sound of a laser shot fizzed through the trees.

'Delta leader, report!'
'I thought I saw something in the trees. I'm going closer to have a look.'

The Alpha team leader turned to his second in command.

"I bet it's just another bird he's seen. That man is jumpier than a frog on acid."

The second in command gave a chuckle with a knowing look.

Ifor watched the Delta leader through his droid. The

man cautiously crept forward making use of the available cover. From behind him the droid slowly descended to within three metres and dropped the leader where he crouched.

'We may have to move a little quicker, boys. They think they've seen something, but they don't know what yet,' Ifor warned.

'Right! Let's pick up the pace. I want all of the guards neutralised ASAP,' Thorn replied.

Twenty two guards and four minutes remained before the defences came back online. The fifteen droids went about their tasks with speed, accuracy and as much stealth as time would allow. The bikes were now just fifty metres from the perimeter, except Yilnar who was still a hundred metres behind.

The signal finally came that the last guard was taken care of and the five men started making their way to their positions inside the complex.

Thorn reached his cover just as his three droids joined him. He scanned the area. In his sight was the building with the extra guards and the transporter landing area. Something wasn't right. A group of guards came out of the building heading for the main domed building.

'Everybody in?'

The four men confirmed their presence. A crackle and a fizz told them the defences were back on.

'I don't like this. It's all been too easy. Did anyone notice anything about those guards that came out of the building?'

'They're just as ugly as the rest of them,' quipped Ifor.

'They don't have their neural bands on. When was the last time any of you saw the TechPsychers without

neural bands?'

'Never. They even keep them on when they have a haircut,' Yilnar said.

'So what's so different about today?' Akarn queried. Before anyone could formulate an answer a blinding flash engulfed them. At the time Thorn thought that it wasn't so much a visible flash, but one that was observed only by the mind and an instant after that, excruciating pain filled the inner most part of his very soul until...

CHAPTER EIGHT

Now

This time Thorn forced his mind awake. He refused to slip back into unconsciousness. He opened his eyes. That same white nothingness greeted him once more. The same aroma of lavender tickled his nose. He could hear noises to his right. Shuffling feet on a hard surface. A soft noise could be heard just above and behind his head. Then the shuffling feet came towards him.

"Thorn...you are awake again."

Thorn turned towards the voice. Memories of the alien form before him came back, but caused him to wince with pain.

"You may feel some discomfort for a while. Your mind has been through a very traumatic experience."

Torst looked up to some instrumentation that glowed in mid-air behind Thorn's head.

"Your signs are looking stronger than they did two days ago."

"How...long...have I been here?"

"Three days. We weren't sure you were going to make it, but against all of the odds you did. Something our Warrior caste would be very interested in if they had the opportunity."

Thorn turned his head back. His mind was trying to drag him back under, but he was a lot stronger now and resisted quite easily.

"What happened? Where am I? Where are my men?"

"All in good time. You need more rest. You are safe here. Can you sit up?"

Thorn could feel the use of his limbs had returned and slowly he managed to move them, but was unable to rise from his lying position.

"No matter. We'll arrange for some physio on your limbs. That's the downside to having organic arms and legs. They cease to work when not used for a long period or if they get damaged."

Torst walked back to the wall at the other side of the room. He stood there for a short while as if he was staring at something on it. Thorn could feel something in his mind as though a static charge was being released on his brain. He screwed up his face in pain. It lasted a few seconds and then receded. Two more alien figures materialised next to Torst.

'So he will need physical rehabilitation as you predicted,' one of them sent.

'Yes, but it shouldn't take long. He has some movement in his limbs,' replied Torst.

'And his mind? Any damage sustained?' sent the other.

'There's been no damage, but there has been a change. As to what this means at this time is hard to predict.'

A long moan of discomfort rumbled from Thorn's lips.

Chark, one of the new aliens, looked almost identical to his colleagues apart from subtle differences in his facial features and the shading on his artificial body. He walked over to Thorn and stood by him.

"Has Torst explained what happened to you yet?"

Thorn turned slightly to look into Chark's eyes. The experience unnerved him for a short while. They were dark and cold and a sadness seemed to have made home there.

"No."

"We picked you up on your home world. Barely conscious. It seems some sort of neural bomb had been detonated in the area. It would have overloaded your mind. From the measurements we detected when it was detonated, you are lucky to be alive let alone be speaking to us. Your brain is, well as you humans would say, a miracle. We have not seen anything like it in any of the species we have studied in the six galaxies we have travelled."

Thorn's heart sank.

"You mean no-one else survived?"

"We were only there for a short time, but we detected no other life signs from your group. I'm sorry."

Thorn was experiencing something he had only felt once before. Most of his life he had protected himself from emotional pain by trusting only a few people after the brutal murder of his parents by the TechPsychers. His men, his friends, were the closest he had to a family. A bond built up over a long period. And now they had been wrenched from his life.

Torst came over to him. He could see the hurt on his

face.

"This will not all be in vein. I believe something will come out of this that will help free your people for good."

Chark caught hold of Torst's arm and turned to him. Thorn felt the static in his mind again, this time a little stronger. Again it receded after a few seconds. He turned his head slowly towards the aliens.

Something caught his eye. Something he hadn't noticed before. On their heads a metallic band stretched from one temple to the other and seemed to be fixed in place. His eyes widened.

"You! You're TechPsychers!" Thorn's instinct was to jump up, but his limbs wouldn't allow it yet. His heart was racing and his mind felt pain once more.

Torst put his hands on Thorn's head and he calmed him down psychically.

'He needs more rest. His mind can't take in what has happened yet. I'll bring him round in two cycles. Come back later. He should be OK by then.'

Chark felt a twinge of disappointment.

'I hope so. The council will be meeting again in three cycles. You should feel privileged to even be considered for this project. It is very rare that so much time would be spent on a species. Are you sure that this human can help us achieve our goal? Especially as the other members of the team are dead.'

'I am sure he can help. Just look at the evidence. It doesn't lie. You said yourself it was a miracle that his mind survived the neural bomb.'

'All the evidence says is that it can repair itself very quickly. That will not help us. Besides he would be of no use to us if he is against us and from what I've seen it

would take another miracle to get him on our side.'

'Come back in two cycles. He will have come round by then and I will explain everything to him. I'm sure he will understand the situation.'

Chark walked over to the third alien in the room.

'No-one is as hopeful about this human as I am, but we can't be wasting our time and resources on mere hope. We need evidence and I dearly hope that when I return you will have some.' The two alien's bodies shimmered and then disappeared.

CHAPTER NINE

The stars glistened over the alien planet. It had been in darkness for the last five months and would continue in darkness for the next two. No human had ever reached this galaxy. Until now.

Beneath the tallest mountain a chamber had been created. Nestled in the chamber a module measuring fifty metres long, twenty five metres wide and three metres high had its existence hidden from the outside worlds. Inside Thorn was perched on his bed. He had been awake for five minutes and found he was able to move his limbs again. When he sat up his mind swam for a short while until it cleared and he could see his surroundings properly for the first time.

A pure white enclosure with minimal, what looked like instrumentation, along the wall opposite. The bed on which he sat was in the middle of the room and at its head a panel with some alien writing on it that was suspended in mid-air. From his observations there was one thing missing. A door!

He slid off the bed keeping a firm hold of the side as his unsteady legs got used to the weight of his body again. Shuffling along the edge of the bed he looked around the rest of the room and found...nothing. The place was completely empty apart from the bed and instrumentations. Thorn suddenly had the uneasy feeling he was in some sort of tomb.

"Hello!" he called out. There was no echo as he would have expected from an empty room and no reply. "Hello!" he tried again even louder. He stood there in silence listening for any signs of life. Nothing! His mind felt sore and a little tired as did his leg muscles. He sat back down on the bed.

A shimmer of a shape caught his eye and Torst materialised before him.

"Hello Thorn. How are you feeling today?"

"Tell me what's going on! Why am I here? Where are my men?"

"Do you not remember anything from the last time you were conscious?"

"I remember that you're one of the TechPsychers. The rest is hazy. What's been happening?"

"I'm afraid you are the only survivor after the detonation of a neural bomb. We picked you up after we detected your weak life signs. You've been here for the last five days recovering."

Memories started to filter back into Thorn's mind as the pain of the loss of his friends took hold.

"Where are the other two? They looked exactly like you."

"Maybe to your primitive human eyes, but our race is varied in its population. You will come to recognise this if your stay is prolonged."

Thorn looked at Torst confused.

"What do you mean prolonged? Why have you got me here?"

"There is a council meeting in one cycle to discuss if you are what we have been looking for. You could be the answer to all of our problems and your own races conflicts providing you are agreeable."

"What problems? Why should I help TechPsychers?"

"Thorn, you have the wrong idea about us, partly. Let me explain. I come from a planet called Vulzeon, two galaxies away from your own. Our race has evolved into a caste system. One a Warrior caste and one a Scientific caste. I and my colleagues belong to the latter caste. We differ in how we interact with other species. The Warrior caste use force to either trade with or dominate other species where as we look for peaceful ways to interact with them.

Until two hundred of your Earth years ago, we complimented each other, making great progress in securing beneficial trade with many other species. Then a change in the leaders of the Warrior caste led to a split between us and eventually, due to their greater force, we were subdued in the influence we had on our future. This led to many of us fleeing our home world.

As a species we value and recognise the power of the mind. As you see we discard the bodies we are born with in favour of this artificial replacement. It is so much more versatile and has none of the weaknesses our original organic bodies had. We created the Neural Enhancer, the band on our heads, to increase our brain power. You see, we have pretty much tapped into everything our minds are capable of. We have created machines that we control with our minds for peace and war, but that is as much as we can do.

On our travels through six galaxies so far, we have only found one species that has the brain capacity, though not yet realised, to outperform all others. Incredible powers could be achieved with the correct guidance. And that is the human species."

Thorn looked stunned. Could it be what he had always felt or was this alien pandering to what he had always sought.

"Once the Warrior caste had realised this, they trod very carefully when dealing with your kind. They knew if they tried to take your planet by force that you would fight until you died. That would have been no use to them. When the opportunity arose for trade with an unscrupulous trader, motions were put in place. For the use of our neural technology, test subjects were sent to our home world where they were used in experiments to try to utilise the extra capacity of their minds. However, it was found that the Neural Enhancers had a limited effect on the average human brain. The Warrior caste was on the verge of giving up and probably destroying the whole of the human race when they discovered what you call the 'Naturals'. Those, such as yourself, were better suited to the Neural Enhancers, but not only that, with manipulative brain surgery the Neural Enhancers could be removed altogether.

They began creating army's that had no equal in the galaxies they travelled. Now there are other species seeking out your race to take advantage of the gift some of you possess. None have made it into your galaxy yet. They have no idea where you are, but it is only a matter of time."

Thorn couldn't believe what he was hearing. His heart

sank. He sat quietly for a while trying to digest everything that Torst had said until his anger finally erupted.

"Lab rats! That's all we've been to you? I thought you were supposed to be the peaceful group in your race! Yet you take our kind and experiment on them trying to create some kind of super soldier. To do what?"

"No, Thorn. This is one of the reasons my race has been split. When the Warrior caste detailed the trade terms with your kind, we vehemently opposed it. At a cost to many lives. Those of us that survived and escaped our planet have been trying to find a way to stop what has been going on. We have been following you and your men for a while. We thought you could be the answer."

Thorn just stared at Torst. No emotions showed on his blue face that could give Thorn a clue as to the validity of his story. A stoic expression was a permanent feature on all Vulzeon's.

Could this all be true? Has the human race been sold out by a man blinded by the lust for power? What could he do? The Psychic Knights were no more. His heart ached as he remembered.

Thorn's anger subsided and was replaced by a helpless resignation. He pulled his knees up to his chest and closed his arms around them. Tears welled in his eyes. He felt a loneliness he had only felt once before. Finally he spoke with a weak voice.

"Looks like I'm no use to you now."

Emotions had been mostly eradicated from Torst's people with the use of the Neural Enhancers and Thorn's show of helplessness was completely ignored.

"Even though our plans involved all of your team, I

believe you still have enough potential to be successful."

Torst activated a Holo-Screen in front of Thorn. Alien symbols appeared.

"The effect of the neural bomb has made changes to your brain." Torst pointed at the symbols. "The changes are significant and by all known information we have on your species, you should be dead. Your brain repaired itself at a colossal rate and preliminary tests show that there is activity in nearly all areas of the brain, although very slight. Can you feel any difference in your mind?"

Thorn shook his head slowly.

"I can feel a little buzzing...no humming, but that's all."

"You need to look deep into your mind. Let me help you." Torst went to place his hands on Thorn's head. Thorn's initial reaction was to pull back, but after Torst explained what he was going to do he relaxed.

As he looked into his own mind a strange new world emerged. At first he felt a swimming, swirling sensation with sadness all around. As he plunged deeper and deeper bright psychedelic colours surrounded him, enveloping him. Though he felt he was falling, it was in a controlled way. The further in he went the sadness subsided a little and the darker it became. The swirling became more violent and he was losing control of his descent.

Suddenly he was thrown from the bed as it flew through the air to the far side of the room crashing against the wall before coming to rest. Thorn was thrown against Torst and they ended up sprawled across the floor.

"What did you do?" Thorn screamed at him as he scrambled backwards until his back hit a wall. If Torst could have felt fear, after touching Thorn's mind, he would have been terrified.

"I did nothing. I merely helped you look into your mind. The rest was all of your doing."

Thorn began sobbing with fear. Torst got up and retrieved the bed with his mind. A moment passed as Thorn calmed down and the tears subsided. Torst helped him back on to the bed.

"Try to describe what you saw," Torst said.

Thorn took a couple of shaky breaths as he tried to recall.

"I felt as though I was falling, at first, but still in control. Everything was so...sad. Then, the deeper I went everything around me became...violent. I tried to reach out to stop myself going any further. Going further into the dark hole below me. I grabbed hold of something, but not with my hands, and threw it at the hole to try to block it and that's when I came round and found myself on the floor."

Torst called up another Holo-Screen and studied the symbols.

"This is like nothing I have seen before. The raw power seems limitless. Can you do anything with your mind at the moment? Anything that you could do before?"

"I couldn't do much before. Move small objects, psych talk with my people. That's all."

A fist sized spherical object materialised in Torst's hand.

"Try to keep this in the air."

Thorn looked at the object in Torst's hand. Suddenly it flew straight up and sat in a dent it left in the ceiling.

"Wow! That is really light." The object slowly came

down to head height.

"Now what I want you to do is squeeze it as hard as you can. Don't worry about breaking it. It's made from an alloy that is the hardest material we know of. I can monitor the pressure you exert on it."

Thorn began to squeeze with his mind. A slight stabbing pain in the recesses of his brain gradually increased until the ball dropped to the floor and he lowered himself onto the bed.

"I can't do any more. I need to rest."

"OK. I will return in a few hours to see how you are doing. When you are rested I will take you above and show you around."

Thorn barely heard the last sentence as he drifted into a deep sleep.

Torst went through the information on the Holo-Screen. The remnants of emotion he had left creased his face in to a wry smile.

"Let's see you dispute this evidence, Chark." The screen disappeared and soon after so did Torst.

CHAPTER TEN

Earth glowed in the orbit of the sun. Its vibrant colours and homely feel could be bettered nowhere else in the galaxy. Oh you could get better climates on the Alpha planet in the Delta system and pleasures unrestricted on Morious in the Beta system, but for pure feelings of being back in the metaphorical womb, you can't beat Earth.

That's how Conrad Preest felt right at this moment. Sat in his rotating apartment just on the coast of Dubai. He lounged in the pool on his balcony looking through the glass wall across the ocean. He loved the ocean. He was brought up on the beach. Two hundred and fifty years ago in a beach hut the size of a small house. The best years of his life. He had money and power now, but for pure happiness he couldn't beat those days and often drifted back to reminisce.

The sun was low on the horizon now and it had been five days since he had finally rid himself of those annoying Psychic Knights. What happened to them now was of no consequence to him. They were out of the picture. Though he was a bit annoyed that the leader had mysteriously disappeared. The last scan of the area showed very little life signs and those that were detected wouldn't have lasted the day.

Still, the rest of the group he had made a tidy profit from or was owed some big favours even though he was sure they wouldn't be alive by now. All in all the untested neural bomb had been a success. Once the rebel's hideout world was found and neutralised he could carry on with the business of expanding his empire across the galaxy. There were only a few hundred worlds left. Most only populated by a few thousand people. It shouldn't take too long.

He sank lower into the water and closed his eyes. The water rippled against his rough features. He was never known as a handsome man and the deep scare on the top of his head that had contributed to the loss of his hair couldn't be passed off as a birth mark. However, now that he had the power there was no shortage of female company.

'If you would just check these results you would see what abilities he has. Far in advance of any other subject we have tested.' Torst was in the main module trying to get Chark to look at the newest results from Thorn.

'I will see your findings when you present them to the council. Until then I have urgent matters to attend to.'

Chark left Torst standing on his own. Chark had sway over the council, something that was always useful. Torst desperately wanted to get him on his side and felt sure once he saw the results he would help in any way he could.

Torst looked around him. The original plain module, from the view of the outsider, was still there. Two kilometres long and one kilometre wide and a height of four metres. The plain white walls looking as though they went on forever. But to Torst and his fellow Vulzeon's, thanks to a device located in the centre module that transmitted to all of their Neural Enhancers, they saw the landscape of their home world. The lime coloured suns in the yellow sky above. The rolling hills covered with the JuJu trees and their fur covered branches.

The courtyard in which he stood was alive with his colleagues discussing everyday matters which usually consisted of talk of the latest subject that showed promise. Everyone knew of Thorn, but viewed him as just another promising specimen that wasn't going to deliver. There was another on their lips at the moment. Not from the human species, but a Leoneon. A biped from Lenois, a planet in the Cenium galaxy. Its brain capacity was only three quarters the size of the humans, but showed promise in a recent study.

The gathering of the council was to discuss the possibility of tutoring Shriln, as he was known, to develop his mind to its full potential. Torst had managed to get an invite to the meeting on the results he had so far. Mostly down to Chark's persuasion, but he seemed to have cooled to the idea of taking Thorn further. What Torst needed was something that would show beyond all doubt that it wouldn't be a waste of time to pursue the humans mind.

The sky above was changing to a deep red. Time for the council to gather.

The ornately carved square building that lay just to the East of the courtyard was a bright red in colour and was big enough to hold a hundred and fifty Vulzeon's, but today it would house just sixty four. Numbers had been depleted due to the capture of several units from the Garian Sector which needed to be started up again with new council members. This happened frequently as the Warrior caste hunted them down and found their hideouts.

Inside the neural projected building was one central room. Lighting was provided by the luminescence of the ceiling which could be controlled by the mind; as most things were. The walls themselves were of a Richter stone with white veins weaving their way through the red grainy surface. It could only be found in the southern hemisphere of Vulzeon due to the vicious cold weather conditions. It was a stone that was synonymous with the Scientific caste.

The wooden flooring was harvested from the praying fields of the religious sect known only as Drionans.

Each of the council stepped into their elevated open cubicles. These cubicles circled a central platform that provided a stage for the hopeful scientist to plead their case.

The cubicles rose into the air to impress the council's authority even more and the edges of the glowing ceiling dimmed to leave just the central platform illuminated. A lonely figure almost identical to Torst stepped in to the light. No words passed his lips, but dialogue began.

'We have two candidates this meeting. One was requested on special merit. The first is Asherst with his findings on the Leoneon.'

Torst was outside the building by the waterfall. His

mind allowed him to feel a cool air blowing across the water. He'd been in front of the council only once before. An experience that he felt lacked the necessary authoritative information required to sway the council in his favour. He left that day with a lower standing amongst his scientific community. He was much younger then and less prepared. That case was more to do with becoming the youngest finder rather than having a viable subject.

Asherst had been inside now for fifteen minutes. Torst had known him most of his life. Starting off as friendly rivals in the Mastering years, Asherst had become bitter, one emotion the Vulzeon's couldn't overcome, and any little victory was a triumph for him. The fact that Torst had gate-crashed this meeting was like a knife in Asherst's back.

Another ten minutes and Asherst emerged from the council meeting. He ignored Torst as he walked by. The Presenter, who showed Asherst out, beckoned Torst towards the door.

'Wait here.'

He turned and re-entered the building leaving Torst at the entrance.

'Now for Torst who, as mentioned before, is here on special merit. He brings the findings on the human.'

The Presenter sent a signal to Torst's mind and he entered, replacing the Presenter on the platform. He stared into the darkness. Nothing could be seen.

'Torst, you stand before us with a special merit to display your findings. Having already seen Asherst and his impressive specimen I urge you to reconsider this meeting. It is very rare two findings are selected.'

Torst thought for a moment. He was up against the

odds now. It seemed they had made their minds up about Asherst and his subject. Why would they consider Thorn? He straightened up his body and calmed his mind.

'It may be rare, but it has happened before. I believe I have found what we have always searched for. This human has far greater potential than I have ever witnessed. I believe he will become everything we need to halt the Warrior caste and their crimes.'

'We have viewed some of your data. He is impressive, but nothing to suggest that what you say will come to pass.'

'I have more data for you to review. I recently took the human into his own mind. The reaction was...uncontrolled, but powerful. Following on from that I gave him the Constriction test.'

A Holo-Screen appeared before him just above his head visible to everyone in the room. A series of symbols rolled across it. A hiss of murmurs filled his mind as the council looked at the results.

'Are these true? They have not been tampered with?'

'They are true. You can run any checks on them you like. The humans mind was drained from the previous experience and so was not at full strength, yet you see he has done what no other mind has done to the constriction ball. Dare I suggest that if he was at full strength the ball would not have survived.'

More murmurings.

'I fear you may be stretching the possibility a little too far to suggest the hardest known material could be destroyed, but you have some compelling evidence for us to consider. We will discuss the merits of your case and notify you of our decision in due course. You are

dismissed.'

The Presenter entered the room and guided Torst out of the building. Now all he could do was wait.

CHAPTER ELEVEN

Thorn was awake and conscious of his surroundings again. In fact he had been awake for some time now. He had feigned unconsciousness to give him time to come up with a plan of escape. Frustratingly, so far he had come up with nothing.

Torst was at the head of his bed going over data on a Holo-Screen.

"Your brain is almost back to full health. How are you feeling?" he asked.

Knowing his thinking time was up he replied.

"A lot better." Thorn sat up and looked around. "You don't go in for much decoration, do you?"

Torst gave what looked like a smile, but it lacked any feeling.

"You'd be surprised at what we see." Torst fell silent again contemplating his next words. "Have you been thinking much about what we discussed last time? I know you have been awake for a while now."

Thorn looked at Torst and felt the anger welling up.

"What, have I been thinking how your race is experimenting on humans and turning them into soldiers to fight wars that are just part of some total domination trip. You're damn right I have. I don't know what's worse, that or the fact that it's a human that's Trafficking his own kind."

"But we can help each other to end what is happening."

"This means I'd have to trust you, which I don't see how I can. On the other hand if I refused would you just dispose of me? Either way I'm not in control of the situation. You're holding all the cards."

"We are not the Warrior caste. We do not dispose of someone if we have no use for them. You would be taken to anywhere you wanted to go."

"Like I said, I have no good reason to trust what you say. For now though I'll go along with your little plan. But I'm warning you, there's no way you're going to cut into my brain."

Torst again tried a smile.

"You have my word, though you do not trust me, that you will not be our guinea pig. If you are selected to begin your Mastering I will show you everything that we do and how we guide you on your path. You can see others who are part way through their Mastering and be assured of your well-being."

Thorn felt the static in his mind once again.

"A decision has been made," Torst said. "We are summoned before the council."

Thorn looked around. "How do we get out? I haven't seen a door yet."

"We use a method similar to your Rejuvenating machines, but far more advanced." With that they both disintegrated into small particles and disappeared.

Thorn found himself in a larger version of the module he had just come from filled with what looked like clones of Torst. It looked as though he was in a world of mime artists. Torst handed him a headband.

"You will need this."

Thorn put it on his head gingerly. Suddenly a whole new world appeared before him. He took a step back in surprise.

"Whoa!"

"Yes, that's the standard reaction when the World Projector is first experienced by non Vulzeon's."

He took the headband off again and was immediately presented with the plain white interior of the module. Again, when he placed the headband back on his head the full beauty of Torst's home world came into view.

"Welcome to my home world. This is a projection of our community as it was about two hundred years ago. I have no idea what it looks like now. We...don't get to go back unless we are captured."

Thorn was too busy taking in his surroundings to notice the almost sadness in Torst's voice. He was captivated with the sights. Mesmerised by the vivid colours. The Torst look-a-likes could now be seen doing things. Nothing that he could recognise as an activity, but it just seemed to fit in the surroundings, looking less like random movements. The bright red building stood out with the darkening sky behind it.

"We must wait over there for the Presenter." Torst pointed to a circled area just outside the entrance to the building. It was ringed with a trough of silver liquid. Two figures were in the circle already. One looked like Torst and the other was reptilian in form and stood at about six foot five inches tall. As they entered the circle the two figures greeted them with what looked like contempt. The static began in Thorn's mind again and the Leoneon looked in discomfort too.

When the Presenter appeared the static increased for a moment before fading away. Thorn caught Torst's shoulder.

"I keep getting a kind of static in my mind."

"Yes, I apologise for that. It's just our way of communicating. It requires some training to be able to understand the subtle nuances. Let me activate the limited function translator." He adjusted something on Thorns headband. *'How's that. This will allow you to understand what's going on. You should be able to speak to me now through your mind. However, if you are ever in front of the council you must never speak.'*

Crystal clear words came into Thorn's mind and he answered,

'OK.'

The four of them followed the Presenter in to the building and on to the central platform.

'We will be brief as we have word that the Warrior caste have discovered our location and will be here in four cycles. Evacuation has begun from the upper modules. In light of our somewhat forced departure from this planet and the evidence you have both brought before us, we have decided to allow both of your candidates to begin the Mastering. You will leave immediately and travel to separate worlds where, in time, your belief in your candidates will hopefully be our eventual saviour.'

Asherst turned to Torst and stared in to his eyes. To Thorn it looked like two paintings looking at each other, but felt there must be something going on in their minds. The Presenter ushered them out of the building and into the circled area.

"What happens now?" asked Thorn.

In answer to his question the four of them dematerialised leaving the remaining Vulzeon's to the task of evacuating the planet.

When Thorn was conscious of his surroundings again Asherst and the Leoneon were gone. He and Torst were standing in a second circle, also surrounded by a trough of silver liquid.

"We are now on one of our space vessels. We will be transported to a safe destination where we can begin your Mastering."

Torst walked towards one end of the spherical room. A Holo-Screen appeared and he studied the symbols on it.

"Our travelling time will be three days."

"What happened to the other two?"

"They are on another ship going to a different destination. We have many safe worlds around the galaxies."

Thorn looked around. Every surface he could see was smooth. Not a console or computer in sight.

"Unfortunately we have nothing for you to sit or lie on. You see with these bodies we need no rest. We do have a levitation field that can relieve the stresses on your body when you need to which you can also use when you need to sleep."

A light shudder could be felt all around and then it stopped suddenly.

"I would show you around, but this is it. We have no elaborate inner workings as your space craft do. We have no need of comfort. Just a space to check navigation." Torst turned away from the Holo-Screen. "I would begin your Mastering now as we have time before we reach our destination, but it is too dangerous in such a small space. Instead I would suggest I connect you to the database that contains the history of my world. You will get a better understanding of us. The time we have is far too short to take it all in, but will be a good beginning for now. At the same time you will gradually learn our language and by the time we arrive will have no need for the translator."

He moved towards one wall and suddenly a section seemed to project outwards in what looked like a spherical bubble that was big enough to envelope Thorn.

"You can assume any position in the field and it will support you for as long as you want."

Thorn positioned himself in the bubble and felt his whole body float in mid-air, but at the same time his body was well supported. As he settled, his mind became immersed in an alien world and culture.

CHAPTER TWELVE

The planet had changed very little in the time he had spent there. Its seasons had come and gone and come again, but the same indigenous plants surrounded the mountain. The same water ran through the rivers.

However, in the context of the world, subtle changes had been made from when they first arrived. Clearings had been created around the mountain. Rocks the size of small houses no longer stood to attention, but lay on the ground as if catching a little shut eye.

There was no volcanic activity. No wondrous creatures that lay waste to these areas. Just two lonely figures, outcasts from their home worlds.

A large module was once again hidden in the depths of a mountain. Torst was at a Holo-Screen trawling through information that had been sent through from the council. He scanned the symbols carefully ensuring he read the message correctly. Quickly the screen disappeared as Thorn materialised in the module.

"I have to leave for a short while. The council has

some important information for us that needs my personal appearance. I will be gone for no more than four days. Though your Mastering is coming to an end it is no excuse for holding back on the training while I am gone. I will prepare a schedule for you which I expect to be completed by the time I get back. Is that understood?" The unexpected interruption caught Torst by surprise.

"Of course. Do you not need me to attend if the information is for us?"

"No, you will remain here. I will brief you when I return."

Torst arrived at Porovian, a world just inside the Kindrian galaxy, just in time to see the meteor shower spectacle. He hadn't had much time to take in any natural wonders for a long time now and it felt good to witness this show as he approached the planet. When he materialised in the central module located deep in an underground cave, the place seemed deserted. This was the hub of all of the council's activities. The centre where plans for the future of his race were made. So many of his kind had been dispersed throughout the galaxies now, it seemed the Warrior caste were winning the battle.

The courtyard stood, as it had on so many other worlds, in the light of the suns. The World Projector could show infinite scenes, but this was the Home world they all wished to return to and so it would remain until they did.

Inside the building the council were waiting, expecting Torst's arrival. He was shown to the central platform where Chark stood waiting in the spotlight.

'It's good to see you Torst. I understand your

Mastering is going well.'

'It's good to see you, Chark. Yes, the human is almost ready. It's been a challenging time.'

A response came from the darkness.

'I hope the challenging times have been worth it. He showed a lot of promise.'

'I must admit that he hasn't progressed as I had hoped, but he will be a valuable addition to our cause.'

'We don't need valuable additions. We need fulfilled potential. The Warrior caste have severely weakened our numbers in the time you have been Mastering. We fear we don't have much time left.' A short pause. *'However, something has come to our attention recently that gives us renewed hope. The four colleagues of your human are still alive. We don't know exactly where, but we have leads to be followed up. We need them found and the five of them brought together. Your original plan was to Master the five. If the neural bomb has had the same effect on their minds as your subject, they may be the force we need. The lack of time now leaves us little options.'*

Torst glared into the void.

'How has this happened? We were so sure there were no more survivors.'

'What matters now is not what has happened in the past, but what will happen in the future. We need this group together again. And soon. The Warrior caste have somehow gained the same information and have bounty hunters out searching for them. We must act now. All the information we have has been sent to your ship. You must leave at once. Our resources have been depleted too much for us to be able to search for them. We must rely on the human and his ability after the Mastering.'

'I'm sure we will have no trouble getting him to search out his friends, but they will be unprepared. The results of their joining are unpredictable without the Mastering. And to convince them of our cause under such circumstances could undo everything we have done with Thorn.'

'That's something we will have to deal with when the time comes. Our main priority now is to find them. Keep us informed of what is happening and we will send further information when we get it.'

The room was bathed in light as the ceiling glowed its brilliance once again. Torst could see the depleted council as they were lowered to the ground. He counted just ten. Chark led him out of the building into the fading light of the suns.

'Asherst finished Mastering the Leoneon some time ago now. He has been successful in fulfilling the Leoneon's full potential. He has begun Mastering another.'

'Can he be the saviour of our race?'

Chark looked at Torst.

'Not alone. Maybe a small army, but we don't have time to get that many to their potential. I think deep down the council feel that bringing the five humans together is our only hope, though they still authorise Masterings in the vain attempt to find an alternative.'

'How have things become this bad since I've been away?'

'We think we are being betrayed, though we have no way of finding out as our resources are stretched to breaking point. It's only a matter of time before the Warrior caste catch up with us all.'

Torst was now standing in the silver ringed circle

outside of the building. The courtyard was deserted. Such a lonely place. He made his farewells not knowing if he would see Chark again. Looking round, the finality of it all took hold as he ascended to his ship. The fate of his race now lay in the organic hands of five humans.

The news was taken as expected. Thorn demanded the information on the whereabouts of his friends and was ready to leave within the hour.

"I can take you as far as your Beta system. The space port there can provide you with transport to take you to the Gamma system where you can find the Helix Cluster. The third planet, Jornaer, is the last known place where Ifor was seen. I then must return to the council. My services are needed there."

Torst produced, what looked like a flat crystal. He placed it on the skin of Thorn's chest.

"This will allow us to communicate across large distances. It also contains all information that we have on your friends. As soon as I get more information I will contact you."

CHAPTER THIRTEEN

On the journey to the Beta system, Thorn chose an appropriate outfit to wear. The attire he wore during his Mastering was not suitable for general day use. He chose an all in one body-suit made from a skin tight material formed from a combination of technologies from four different galaxies. It provided protection from all hand to hand combat weapons. It was one of many outfits he had designed over the years.

A knee length, leather style coat that was impervious to steel blades and absorbed laser fire and lightweight boots that contained a surprise in the sole completed the outfit. He secured a belt around his waist from which he hung his laser sword. He had grown his hair over the years and it now hung down to his shoulder blades. A style that reminded him of his favourite comic character from childhood; the Star Rider.

Torst left him in the docking bay of the space port. No long goodbyes. Just a quick shake of the hands and a wishing of good luck, a custom Torst had learned years earlier from Thorn.

His ship glided out of the docking bay and disappeared into the distance until a bright light signalled his jump into hyperspace leaving Thorn looking after it. A strange sense of loss crept over him until he shook his head and turned away.

The space dock was, at the time, a first collaboration between humans and a mixture of alien races. The elaborate station was co-owned and built with three other races found in this system. The Druans, very similar to humans, but their physiology was completely different. The Erronians, a bipedal species with colour changing skin and the Pertruans who had ape like features, less hairy and with the strength of ten men. The place was loosely run by a combination of the three, but it seemed the laws were only enforced when no resistance was offered.

Thorn walked through the waiting area which was big enough to get two cargo ships in and eyed the bars and eateries that ran around the periphery. It had been a long time since he had had a drink. 'Maybe I'll pop in when I've sorted transportation out,' he thought to himself.

He walked over to the nearest information kiosk to be confronted by a Druan looking droid.

"How may I help you," came the deep voice, a characteristic of the Druans.

"I'm looking for transport to Jornaer in the Gamma System."

"I'm afraid you can no longer arrange transport from here. Can I help you with anything else?"

"Where can I arrange transport?"

"It is now illegal to arrange transport from this station?"

A gruff looking Pertruan was passing.

"Where are you looking to go human?"

Thorn turned to face him.

"Jornaer in the Gamma System."

The alien looked around as if checking that no one was listening.

"It'll cost you," he whispered.

"I have credits."

He looked Thorn up and down then took in a deep breath as though he was sniffing him.

"Follow me."

They both headed off to a bar on the next level of the waiting area. Inside it was sparsely lit. A contrast to the bright waiting area. On the tables were glow lamps that gave a seductive ambiance. He noticed two humans, looking a little scared, at a table with two Druans.

Thorn was led to an alcove set into the far wall. The force field engaged behind them giving them complete privacy.

"We're safe from prying eyes and prying minds now. You can't be too careful. The TechPsychers want to know everyone's business. Now, how many credits do you have?"

Thorn wanted more information. Torst had told him to be careful when mind probing someone as there were detection units now at all major stations that could detect any mind activity. The TechPsychers were doing their best to eradicate all natural psychers.

"Why is it illegal to get transportation from here?"

The Pertruan looked quizzically at him.

"Have you never been here before?"

"Not for some time. I've been away."

"Well your TechPsychers seem to be running the

show here now. This seemed to be a major meeting point for escaping natural psychers from your Home world. One way for them to stop this was to outlaw their only escape route. Pretty much killed our lucrative sideline. You're not one of them are you?"

"What if I am?"

"You'll never get off of the station. They have scanners to detect any abnormal brain activity as you leave. There are TechPsychers all over the place mind probing whenever they want. I'm surprised you've got this far without being detected. Unless you're not one of them. Now why would you lie about something like that?"

One of the techniques Thorn learned during his Mastering was a way to mask his ability by training his mind to only show normal human brain activity. It was a kind of filter that only allowed that activity be shown.

"I never said I was one of them."

"No, I don't suppose you did. In that case human, the price is three hundred credits. I will be leaving in three hours. Now why don't you buy me a drink to seal the deal?"

Thorn smiled.

"Of course. My name is Thorn. What can I call you?"

"Once you pay me you can call me anything you like, but until then I am Enyar." The yellow teeth seemed to clash with Enyar's skin colour as he smiled. "That name sounds familiar. Have you been around the Beta System much?"

"No, I've been...incommunicado for some time now."

Thorn pulled out his credit chip card and scanned it across the table. A holo-image of a human head appeared.

"What can I get you to drink?" it said.

"I'll have an Earth World rum with ice and..." He looked over to Enyar who said.

"A Pertruan Childra."

Both drinks appeared on the table within seconds. The Pertruan Childra glowed its green luminescence and lit up Enyar's face. Picking up the glasses they then clinked them together and proceeded to drink. Thorn screwed up his face as the drink washed over his taste buds and down his throat.

"That's either a poor quality rum or my liking for the drink has changed over the years."

Enyar chuckled at the look on Thorn's face.

CHAPTER FOURTEEN

Outside of the alcove a commotion began. It was muffled by the force field, but loud enough to interrupt the two.

"Sounds like the TechPsychers are in."

"Can we release the field? I want to see what's going on," said Thorn. As the field disappeared and he saw once again the sight of a human with a headband torturing an innocent person, a familiar feeling of hate filled his soul. Tempered, but still there. He had to check himself to stop from squashing the three men to a pulp.

What they were doing was obvious and he could feel it. The two humans he spotted when he entered the bar had been thrown across the room. They were being mind probed with no care for any damage that was being done. The two Druans were being held in the air by one of the TechPsychers mind. Thorn could feel the scratching and scraping happening to the minds of the two humans. He felt the agony they were going through.

Torst had stressed to him that he had to stay away

from trouble, but he couldn't let them go through this any longer. He threw out two barriers to the suffering men preventing further damage to their minds. The two TechPsychers reeled back a little.

"Wow! This one's a strong one," one of them said.

"Yeah, this one too."

They tried harder to get a hold of their victim's minds. The harder they tried the more painful it got until they both broke their links.

The Naturals laid on the floor bemused by what was happening. The pain in their heads had suddenly ceased. Thorn turned to Enyar.

"I need for us to leave in thirty minutes and we will have two more passengers."

"I...I can't. I have things to do. Supplies to buy. You're not thinking about taking those two? It's too dangerous. We'll never get them onto the ship."

"I'll pay you ten times the price you quoted. Don't worry about getting them on the ship. Leave that to me. All I need is three crew uniforms. Leave them at the information kiosk."

The lure of the price was very tempting for Enyar. He'd never seen that sort of credit before. He'd been in more dangerous situations than this before and for less credit. But the TechPsychers! That's a different matter.

"I need an answer soon Enyar," Thorn stressed.

Going against his better judgement Enyar blurted out, "OK. We can pick up supplies en route. The ship's in bay forty eight." He slipped out the front door avoiding the baffled TechPsychers.

As soon as he left Thorn slipped off of his chair and was behind the first TechPsycher in an instant. He swept him and as he fell backwards Thorn jumped up with a kick to his chest. In mid air a Laser knife hummed to life from the end of his boot and pierced the TechPsychers heart killing him instantly. A spinning back kick scythed the second TechPsychers head from his shoulders.

During this time Thorn kept a hold of the third with his mind, holding him in the same position until he was right beside him. The two Druans had dropped to the floor and disappeared as soon as they could get to their feet. Thorn could now hear the concerns from the control centre through the headband.

'Franks, are you close to the Sipid Bar? The scanners are going crazy.'

Thorn replied as Franks.

'Yeah, nothing going on up here. They must be playing up again. Get one of the droids to take a look.'

'OK, but have a scout around to be sure.'

'Will do.'

Thorn cut off the communication. Pulling the laser sword from his belt he dropped the TechPsycher to the ground, lifeless. He leapt over to the two Naturals on the floor.

"We have to be quick. I'm going to place a filter in your mind to stop the scanners detecting you and then I'll quickly make you feel more relaxed so we can get out of here without rousing suspicion. At the moment you both look like you're about to be executed. I've got a ship waiting for us."

"Who are you?" one of them asked.

"Don't worry about that now. Just try to relax for a moment."

As Thorn entered their minds the physical change was noticeable. Their bodies relaxed and loosened up. The muscles on their faces eased and expressions of contentment appeared. Thorn finished and went over to the TechPsychers bodies. He produced a device that he strapped to his hand and then laid it on one of the bodies. It immediately disintegrated leaving a pile of dust on the floor. The other two followed quickly. Thorn turned to an onlooker.

"Can you arrange for this to be swept up?"

Within seconds the cleaning droids were out on the floor sweeping away the remains of the TechPsychers.

"Let's go," said Thorn to the two Naturals.

The three of them walked out of the bar leaving the customers carrying on as if nothing had happened and without a shred of sympathy for the TechPsychers. Thorn scanned the area outside with his eyes. Everyone going about their business. He caught sight of Enyar handing over a bag to the information droid and then hurriedly walking away.

"Stay close to me and try not to catch anyone's eye, especially the TechPsychers."

They leisurely made their way down to the lower floor and then to the information kiosk. A small queue had formed in the time it took for them to get there, but vanished within a few minutes.

"My employer left a bag for me. His name is Enyar and I am Thorn."

"Yes sir. It's right here." The droid handed over the bag. "Can I help you with anything else?"

"No, this is all, thank you."

The three then found a deserted area to change in. Within minutes they were dressed in the uniforms of transportation crew members. Thorn made sure they were alone before speaking.

"Now I need you to stay calm just a little while

longer. We have two checkpoints to get through and I'm not sure how long the filter in your minds can last. It's the first time I've had to do it on someone else so we're flying by the seat of our pants here. Do you both understand what's going on?"

They both nodded in a spaced out kind of way.

"You're here to save us," one of them said with a smile.

"Hmm. Maybe I relaxed you too much. Can't worry about that now. Let's go."

They made their way to the first checkpoint situated just below the bar they had just come from. Two TechPsycher guards stood menacingly by the exit. Thorn let the two Naturals go through first and followed closely behind. They went through the same time as a small group of Pertruans, who by the look of it had been in the bars since they had arrived. One of them was shepherding them through. Suddenly the group stopped and a luminous liquid came gushing out of the Pertruan at the front of the group. So forceful that it splashed up and onto one of the TechPsychers.

"What the...? You dirty, stinking..." A mind-burst threw the Pertruan across the floor. The group started to get rowdy until three more TechPsychers joined in and eventually calmed the situation. By the time everything was quiet, Thorn and the Naturals were making their way down the long corridor to the docking bays. They caught up with another group when they got to the second checkpoint.

This time a single TechPsycher manned the exit. He was more concerned with making sure there were no problems with the ships getting away and liaised with the control centre in the module far above them. The group stopped by him and engaged in a conversation. Thorn squeezed past the group being as inconspicuous as possible.

Dock forty eight was a good half a mile along the docking area. A disembarkation pod stood idly waiting for a customer. The three entered and sat down.

"Your destination please," came the voice from the speaker in the roof.

"Dock forty eight."

The door closed behind them and they started moving. Halfway to their destination the pod slowed to a halt.

"We have been detained by the security. Please remain seated," came the voice.

"Why have we stopped?" asked one of the Naturals calmly.

Thorn got up to look out of the window.

"I don't know. Let me check your filtering before they come." He once again entered their minds and re-enforced the barriers that he had put in place.

A second pod stopped alongside them and two TechPsychers got out. They opened the door and looked inside. The headbands glinted in the pods lights. The two men looked menacing in their dark uniforms with their laser guns in their hands. Their faces were no more inviting than their overall look.

"We had unusual readings on our scanners when you went through. We'd just like to check you over." Without waiting for a reply one of the men produced a portable scanner and started waving it around the pod.

"Everything's fine in here. You can continue on your way." As soon as they left, the pod continued. Thorn let out a relieved sigh.

CHAPTER FIFTEEN

The Shafian, the transport for Thorn and his two new additions, was a class C ship. Built for one thing and that was for moving all kinds of waste products to and from neighbouring galaxies. One race's waste is another race's Granium, as Enyar's old Captain used to say to him. At the time Enyar thought he had been travelling the stars for too long and inhaling the fumes from the containers in the hold, but soon came to realise how true these words were.

The luxuries that the Captain enjoyed in his quarters were what the leaders on his home world were accustomed to. There was no need to leave the ship. Everything was there. Enyar knew then what he wanted. And when the Captain handed over the business to him, he got exactly that.

Things were good until the TechPsychers showed up. Strangling the profit out of the business. Enyar knew nothing else and so was stuck with scrabbling around for any business going. This particular trip he was hauling

Terulium, a waste product from the fourth mining planet in the Pion System. As waste products go, this was the most useless. It gave off a smell so bad that if you were exposed to it for too long your screwed up facial features would stay in that position for the rest of the day.

And it was also the most dangerous. The fumes were so unstable that the hold had to be vented into space at regular intervals leaving a trail behind the ship like a whipping purple tail. The only way to dispose of it was into the sun in the Gamma system. No mean feat with a ship as big as this one.

Enyar sat at his table in his quarters chomping away on an Epoua bone. Thorn and the two Naturals, Tianu and Saul, had just finished their food. Enyar was regaling them with tales of some of his trips and the things he'd seen.

"...and it just exploded in his hand taking off all eight fingers. I tell you now, that was one of the funniest things I've ever seen." He cackled with laughter and some meat fell from his mouth onto the floor. A small creature, the size of a squirrel, scuttled across the floor and devoured the morsel. This was Enyar's pet Chriln.

"So, Tianu, Saul. Where were you off to before you were invited on our little trip?" He gave a wry smile to Thorn who responded in kind.

Tianu spoke first.

"We were going to Prius 3. It's a safe planet for people like us."

Thorn immediately shot him a glance.

"Used to be," said Enyar. "If it's the same Prius 3 I'm thinking of it was destroyed about six months ago."

"What do you mean destroyed?" Thorn's eyes demanded an answer.

"Well when I say destroyed I mean it was terraformed. Completely changed the face of the planet. It's big news when something like that happens. It's very rare for a whole planet to be terraformed."

"What happened to the people on it?"

"I don't know. Up until now I thought the planet was uninhabited." Enyar was a little shook up by Thorn's reaction. "Did you know the people there?"

There was a pause before Thorn spoke.

"It was my home world after I left Earth."

"Had you been away from it for some time then?" asked Enyar.

"Thirty two years. Too long!"

Another pause. Saul spoke first.

"I know who you are!"

Thorn shot him a glance. Enyar sat up straight and put his bone down.

"Who is he boy? Ever since I heard your name it's been niggling me. I recognise it, but can't place it."

"He is Thorn of Prius 3. Leader of the most successful group of Naturals to have ever lived. He is the leader of the Psychic Knights. The saviour of thousands of Naturals all over the galaxy."

Enyar slammed his fist down on the table.

"Of course! That's where I've heard the name from. It was always on the lips of the TechPsychers in the bars back then. There was always tales of how they survived an attack by your group or how they nearly captured you. Boy, you really were a pain in their backsides. I thought you were killed back on Earth?"

"Not quite."

"Where have you been all this time? And the rest of your group? Are they still around? Are you going to wreak havoc on the TechPsychers again?"

Thorn shot to his feet.

"Our struggle was to free innocent people from the human trafficking that was happening that provided the scum of the human race profit and power. Only this time I am here to end it once and for all." As he turned and left his chair fell to the ground.

"Whoops! Put my foot in it again. Will I never learn?" Enyar turned to Saul. "So what can you tell me about this guy? Have I got to worry about him?"

"Only if you cross him. All I know about him is the stories that we were told when we were younger. The heroics he and his men performed in the name of justice. The hope that he gave to all of us. Of all of the things I've heard, nothing was told of the feeling I get from him."

"And what would that be?" Enyar said picking up his bone again.

"Loneliness and a deep darkness. Something I am very afraid of."

Tianu nodded in agreement.

Enyar stopped with his mouth clamped round his bone. He pulled it away slowly.

"Then I should be worried about him. Is he likely to bring trouble?"

"Only to those who deserve it...and to himself."

"You and your cryptic answers. As long as he pays me I'll be gone after I drop you all off at Jornaer. He's lucky I need the credits or I would ditch him at our next stop." He continued with his meal, but didn't enjoy it as much.

The Shafian docked in the station orbiting the planet

Alshun. The crew went about arranging for supplies while Enyar, Tianu and Saul stayed on the ship. Thorn travelled to the surface. During the trip to Jornaer he had contacted Torst who gave him a lead on where Ifor could be. Apparently he was acting as some sort of mercenary selling his services to any low life with credit and the last place he had acted for someone was on Alshun.

It wasn't by luck that Enyar stopped here for supplies. A little thought manipulation on him made him change his mind from his original destination.

Alshun was a spent planet. Mined until it was empty of the ore that was used for building dwellings on the nearby planets. It was now a stopping off point before moving onto the Fedora system, a system that attracted the well off and Alshun entertained them before they moved on.

Because of this the main city housed supply companies and the bars housed swindlers. TechPsychers had a loose control of the place. No checkpoints or scanners were employed here yet. Just a lax security that threw its weight around every now and then.

The information that Thorn was given was about a company that hadn't been taken over by the TechPsychers yet. It was a clothing company that provided the finest materials in all of the System. Clothes that were tailor made for you while you waited or they would be waiting for you at your destination.

Thorn made contact with the owner just before they arrived. He made himself out to be a wealthy businessman and wanted clothes for his large, extended family on Drayloon in the next System. The meeting was arranged for two hours after they arrived.

CHAPTER SIXTEEN

Thorn was directed to the heart of the city where his meeting would take place; the part of the city that displayed some opulence. The walkways were lined with Crystalline marble that glittered in the sun. The liquid Platinum lamps lit the shop fronts at night, constantly flowing up and down their form. There were no market traders on these streets. No food stalls selling processed meat made into edible shapes. A constant vigil was kept by Crystal cameras that would just as much cut you down with a laser beam than let you break any of the rules that had been formed by the shop owners.

The sound of a harp played as the shop door opened signifying the arrival of a customer. A tall, scrawny being appeared. A little taller than Thorn, but with a physical weakness that was immediately apparent. The Alshunians were of a similar shape to humans, but with features that resembled a combination of creatures from Earth. Ears of a dog, eyes of a cat, tongue of a snake, nose of a badger. A living collage. He greeted Thorn with his hand extended.

"Trurn Bishop?"

Thorn took his claw like hand with a smile acknowledging the name.

"That's right! You must be Plion."

Plion was a local. He was the son of wealthy parents who lived at the heart of the city, close by, among the elite of the Alshun world. A life that he had shunned from an early age to set up his business, which ironically had now made him wealthy.

There was a pause as Plion looked Thorn up and down. His yellow eyes scanning the whole of Thorn's body.

"Forgive me. We don't get many Earthers out this far. Please, follow me."

Thorn followed the Alshunian through the doorway to the right. Something was odd about the flowing robes he wore. The ends of the robes were floating about two inches from the floor, but Thorn couldn't see what was holding them up.

"Would you like a drink? I'm afraid I don't have any Earther drinks. The nearest I have is something called Armuk. It's a spirit that is mixed with water."

"That will be fine."

The room they were in was bathed in sheets of lavishly coloured cloths laid out on tables and hanging from specially built racks along three walls.

"Please, take a seat. Enjoy my hospitality before the business begins." Plion clapped his hands and two scantily clad Alshun women came into the room carrying trays of food which they laid out before them. The pearlescent scaly skin of the two females glowed in the sunlight that streamed through the large glass roof.

"I have delicacies from all over this System. I'm sure you would have come across some of them before. If not then you are in for a treat my friend."

Thorn looked at the selection of meats and breads and fruits laid out on the plates and savoured the mixture of sweet and spicy aromas that delicately played on his senses. Picking a few he devoured them instantly. He nodded with a smile.

"You are right. This is a treat. I have never tasted anything as sweet and succulent as these meats. Your chef serves you well." He continued eating, savouring each mouthful. Though he was fed well during his exile, his taste buds had never come into contact with anything like the sensations he was enjoying now. The food just melted on contact with his tongue and left an imprint of what could be described as the culinary version of Heaven.

Plion couldn't hold back any longer.

"I have to ask," he said. "Your coat. I've never seen a material like it before. Where does it come from?"

Thorn finished the fruit that was in his mouth before answering.

"I'm not sure. It was given to me as a leaving gift."

Plion got up from his chair and ran his hands over the coat.

"It feels soft and very light, but I get the feeling it is very strong. Maybe strong enough as a protective barrier. Something someone who sees a lot of trouble would wear." His face suddenly dropped and he pulled his hands away. Moving back to his chair the tone in his voice changed.

"Who are you? You haven't come for clothing. You are no businessman. Why are you here?"

The fruit dropped from Thorn's hand onto the plate.

"You are right. I have come here for another reason. I understand you enlisted the services of a human named Ifor a while back. I wish to do the same and need to know how to contact him."

"I don't know what you are talking about."

Three hefty Alshunians came in the door behind Thorn. Despite their size they made no sound as they entered the room. Thorn was immediately aware of them. Not showing that he knew of their presence, he continued.

"My sources tell me..."

"Your sources are wrong. Now will you kindly leave or I'll have my colleagues escort you out of the building."

The three huge figures moved towards Thorn. Instantly they stopped, unable to move, confusion on their faces, the part of their brain that controls movement paralysed.

"I can assure you my sources are not wrong."

"What's the matter with you three? Get rid of him now!"

"They won't be moving for a while. Not until you tell me what I want to know."

"What have you done to them? Who are you? Are you a TechPsycher? No, you don't have a headband. Unless you're a new breed that has no need for headbands."

"I'm not a TechPsycher. I just want to know how to contact Ifor."

Plion slumped into his chair shaking.

"I don't know how to contact him directly. He contacted me. He's not the sort of person you walk up to in the street and ask to do a job for you. I just kept asking about him in the bars on Jornaer and Hellion the main space dock and eventually two of his crew turned up and arranged a meeting."

Thorn got up from his chair and walked behind the three hulks. Suddenly they lurched forward as if an invisible wall had been removed.

"Thank you for your assistance. I'll see myself out."

As he turned and walked through the doorway one of the big men pulled his gun and fired. The red laser bolt seared through the air to within two inches of Thorn's head and stopped dead. Thorn stopped and turned to face the three inch long red strip of light hanging in the air. The gunman gasped as his gun was gradually forced towards him and jammed in his open mouth.

"All it would take is one little thought and you would have a big hole in your head. Now I suggest you don't try that again and don't follow me."

Thorn moved his head to the side and the laser bolt flew passed and left a burnt hole in the wall. The gun dropped out from the gunman's mouth and he dropped to his knees trembling. The other two backed away. Thorn walked towards Plion who sank further into his seat. Stopping at the table he picked up some meat.

"You'll have to give me your recipe some time." He gave a little smile and left the shop.

CHAPTER SEVENTEEN

The craft glided down onto the landing platform with its lights flashing. The journey had taken Conrad Preest nearly three weeks which was one reason he never made it that often, but the visit was prompted by a concerned Insha.

The greeting party guided Conrad to the room where the leader of the Warrior caste waited. Conrad was in awe of the surrounding architecture on route. He had studied pictures and models back on Earth ever since he had first visited Vulzeon, but nothing could replace the feeling of seeing it in the flesh. The soft edges and lines that made up a myriad of shapes that were the decoration on each building continued on inside and pleased the eye so much that it mesmerised Preest as he walked by.

Both Insha and Preest greeted each other with the ceremonial hand gestures of the Warrior caste. Conrad prepared his mind as much as he could for the ensuing conversation. Many times before he had held talks through the use of his headband, but each time it didn't get any easier.

'Greetings Conrad Preest. Welcome to our world once again. I wish it was under different circumstances.'

Insha was an imposing figure. The size of his artificial body was to portrait power and standing within the Warrior caste and allowed him to dress modestly for the visit of his guest. He wore a plain beige, knee length, sleeveless shirt with a thin collar around his long neck.

He was waiting in a large, opulent room decorated with fine art paintings and statues that depicted great battles throughout the galaxy. Conquered races that Preest had never seen before.

'Thank you for the hospitality and the opportunity to see your world again.' Conrad struggled to form the words in Insha's language.

Insha guided him to a chair and sat beside him.

'We have had some very disturbing reports from our scouts. While out searching for the renegades of our home world we have come across news of a Natural that we thought you had rid us of. Thorn, it seems, has been alive and well for the last thirty years and been training with one of our renegades. Now by the unsurprised look on your face you know of this already.'

Preest nodded with a weak smile. *'I have only recently found out myself. However, on the journey here I had word that he had been found and we are keeping a close eye on him.'*

'This man Thorn could be dangerous to you...to us if he has reached his full potential during his training.'

'I'm sure that's not the case. You have been trying yourself for a lot longer and no one has come close to what you think can be achieved.'

Insha paused a moment. *'I hope you are right.*

However it would be wise to eliminate this man to be sure. To help you we have a selection of mind weapons that we have developed over the years. These will kill or incapacitate depending on how strong your foes mind is. I have arranged for some training on their use for you and shipments are being loaded onto your ship as we speak. We have also made enhancements to the neural bands and the data will be uploaded to your ship before you leave.'

'Very good. I will have him taken care of immediately. How is our last delivery of Naturals? Are they performing as you had hoped?'

'It is too soon to tell. We have some experiments to perform before we can decide whether to continue with their physical enhancements. Previous shipments that are serving our needs in a number of galaxies at the moment have impressed, though still nowhere near the full capacities of their brains.'

The two locked in conversation for another hour before Preest and a few of his officers were taken through the intricacies of the weapons. It was a full three hours later before he was sat in his luxurious quarters on his ship heading back to Earth. He summoned his Commander in Chief. A thick set man with short, dark hair and bushy moustache that was braided at the ends.

"I want you to contact our man in the field and tell him to stick with Thorn. We need to know how many of the other bastards are still alive before we terminate him."

It was just by chance that Preest had found out about Thorn. An insignificant report of a disturbance on one of the minor space ports was brought to his attention by one of his officers who thought he recognised Thorn in the surveillance footage. It felt like an old enemy had risen from the grave. Although it couldn't have been worse news, at least he was prepared for the meeting with Insha and a mask of control of the situation could be worn.

"And the weapons? What do we do with them?"

"We have a couple of facilities full of Naturals that we can test them on. Your men will need the practice. Get a team together when we are back on Earth and prepare them to get rid of Thorn for good."

CHAPTER EIGHTEEN

Jornaer was just two days travel from the edge of the Helix System. It glowed from the red sun's light that bounced off of the thick atmosphere that enveloped the planet. A number of space ports were dotted around the planet providing access to various cities. The TechPsychers hadn't reached this far yet and so the planet was a haven for anyone and anything that wanted to get away from them.

The Jornaerns themselves were of humanoid form with a Neanderthal appearance and both males and females stood at around six feet five tall. The planet had been arranged into seven cities divided by large wastelands. The idea was to provide a completely different way of life to one another giving inhabitants the option to change their lifestyle whenever they wanted.

The Shafian glided into the nearest space dock and the clamps secured it to the station. The crew went about their tasks leaving Enyar and his first mate to fill out all of the required data fields on the station masters computer for their stay.

"Wow! That's a big ship you've got there. Looks as though it's seen better times though. I hope it's not going to break away leaving half of it in our clamps." The station master gave a wry smile and the two helpers behind him giggled like little school girls.

"Don't you worry about that. She's as solid as this planet." Enyar finished tapping in his details and paid the docking fee. "When's the next shuttle due to leave?"

"Whenever you are ready. We have a few still in dock. Why don't you stay a while? We have plenty of bars and gambling dens. We're not bound by laws up here. Pretty much anything goes. No matter how depraved."

The station master gave a slow wink as he said this. His sparkling cloak glittered in the intense lights that shone down from above. One thing Jornaer was known for was the brightness across the planet. So much so that visitors had to wear special glasses to protect their eyes. The internal lighting reflected this as the pupils in the Jornaerns eyes were very narrow.

Enyar raised his eyebrows behind his glasses.

"That won't be necessary, thank you. We won't be staying long. We're here to drop somebody off and then we'll be on our way."

"Pity! I know someone who could do things to you that would blow your mind. And she does like a Pertruan. She knows where your Visiv gland is and you know what that would mean." The station master smiled as he saw the look of embarrassment on Enyar's face.

Enyar turned and quickly made his way back to the ship to the distant laughter of the three Jornaerns.

"What's the plan?" Saul was sitting next to Tianu on the observation deck as Thorn entered.

"What do you mean?"

"What do you want us to do when we get on to the planet?"

Thorn shook his head.

"No, you're both staying here. I've arranged with Enyar to find out where the inhabitants of Prius 3 went and to drop you off there."

"But we owe you and if you're going to search for a needle in a haystack, it's better to have three people searching rather than one."

Thorn couldn't argue with that. It was true that his task ahead was going to be difficult considering the size of the planet. He paused.

"OK. You can help, but as soon as we have found him I want you to go with Enyar to find your new home."

Both Saul and Tianu sat bolt upright with big smiles on their faces.

"We'll have him found in no time, you'll see."

"I hope you're right. The sooner we do the sooner we can find the others. OK, the first thing we need to do is find us some place to stay. We'll check with the station master here. Then this station is as good a place to start. There are plenty of bars around here that's likely to attract people who would have heard of Ifor. We need to put it about that we need his services."

"What do we do if someone who knows Ifor makes contact with us?" Tianu could hardly contain his excitement.

"Nothing. Just let them know you're working for someone who wants a meet. Are you able to sense when someone is lying?"

Both of them nodded.

"Good, then if you feel you have a genuine contact give them these." Thorn handed over two small devices. The two young men looked at them quizzically, turning them round in their hands trying to figure out what they were. "They are psychic communicators," Thorn said in reply to the unanswered question. He pointed to a small button on one side of the device. "You press this to activate it and talk into it like you would any other communicator. However, this is tuned to a frequency that I can pick up with my mind and transfer my answers to the users mind."

Saul and Tianu nodded their understanding.

Heavy footsteps announced the arrival of Enyar and his first officer. An unfamiliar look shaped his face that Thorn couldn't tell if it was disgust or embarrassment.

"The sooner I'm away from this place the better as far as I'm concerned. The whole feel of the place makes me uneasy."

"There's been a small change in our plans. Saul and Tianu will stay with me and help me look for Ifor. When he is found and you return they will join you and continue with the original plan."

"OK. How soon can I go?"

"Let us find somewhere to stay first. I'm going to check with the station master for a place in Chaulk as it's our first stop. You two wait here while I'm gone. We'll start looking when I get back."

Thorn had left his firearms on the ship. He didn't want to aggravate anyone while he was here. While learning the customs of the planet he discovered that carrying a weapon was preferable, though diffusing a situation was as good a weapon as any that he had in his armour.

The station was just like any other that he had ever visited. A vast central hub that all docking ports led to. Lining this hub were bars and eateries going up four levels. The floors above this were quarters for resting and sleeping for the ten thousand or so inhabitants of the station or for the travellers that never visited the world below.

The eye protectors he used covered his eye sockets completely and prevented anyone from seeing his eyes. This also prevented him from seeing out, but in situations such as this he much preferred to see with his mind. He had developed a much clearer picture of his surroundings when his vision was impaired in some way. Although this did drain him to the degree that he could only last a day before having to completely rest for two or three days afterwards.

He found the station master from the directions Enyar had given him.

"Well, well, well. If I'm not mistaken, you my friend are from Earth," said the station master in a raised voice. "It's a rare occasion when we see one of your kind. And from my scanners I see you are unarmed. You are either very foolish or very brave."

Thorn raised his head pretending to look up at him. He could see around him that there were now onlookers alerted by the station masters voice. He replied in a calm, quiet voice.

"I have no weapon because I am not here for trouble. I require a residence for myself and two friends down on Chaulk."

The station master looked down into Thorns eye

protector.

"I see you have your eyes hidden."

"I have very sensitive eyes."

"I find you can tell a lot about a species by their eyes and am very suspicious when I can't see them."

"I assure you I am hiding nothing. If you have a darkened room I can remove my protector for you to see. I am just here to find somewhere to stay and maybe sample the hospitality that you have on this station."

The tall Jornaern came from behind his desk and walked around Thorn. As he did his large nostrils flared while he sniffed the scent around him. Thorn saw what was coming next and went with the flow. The slap on his back jerked him forward almost toppling him over.

"Then you've come to the right place Earth man. I have access to the finest living quarters on the whole of Jornaer. And I know all of the best places that a man like yourself would enjoy."

Thorn returned to the Shafian having secured living quarters and a list of bars to visit on the station. Enyar had found some clothes for Saul and Tianu to wear that would help them blend in more until they got down to the surface where they could purchase more suitable attire.

"Until two months time then, my friends. I wish you luck on your search and may Hoolash protect you on your quest."

The three left the ship and headed for the bars as the Shafian glided out of the docking area.

CHAPTER NINETEEN

The walkways were buzzing with life. From all over the galaxy they had travelled. Whether to find a better life, to find their fortune or to escape from something or someone. Thorn didn't recognise half of the beings there, but somehow knew everything about them. A benefit from the stasis field he had spent time in while travelling on Torst's ship.

He was on his own now having instructed Saul and Tianu on what to do and how to act in this place. They had arranged to meet down on the main concourse in a couple of hours.

He remembered well the places he was about to visit. He hadn't been here before, but a bar was a bar no matter what end of the galaxy it was. Drunks in the corner, groups of loud mouth youths who were just old enough to visit these places and sometimes you may find a couple on a date.

The first place he entered seemed like most of the places on the floor and had some kind of music streaming out of the doors and windows. The sounds stopped about six feet from the entrance, as it did in other bars, to stop it annoying passers-by. Not the sort of thing he would listen to, or understand if he didn't know deep in his mind that it was from a planet in the Delta System.

Inside it was darker. Enough for him to remove his shades, but he left them on. High tables were dotted around the centre of the room and long rows of tables lined the walls. The temperature had increased as well. Quite a bit. No doubt the owner felt more at home in this heat than in the cooler air outside as he was from Pent, a planet much closer to a sun than Jornaer.

The place wasn't busy at all. A handful of customers dotted around enjoying the music and drink. Thorn walked over to the bar and was greeted by the Pertruan serving.

"Welcome to Thrush. The best bar on the Station. What can I get you?"

Obviously the Pertruan had no idea what Thrush meant on Earth.

"Do you have Earth rum?"

"Ah. An Earther. No. We don't get much call for it here. How about Jornaern Sholn mixed with the juice from a Ween fruit?"

"OK. I'll try that."

The Pertruan mixed the drink and passed it to Thorn. The sweet smell of the drink floated up into his nostrils as he took a sip. He was expecting a sickly sweet taste going by the aroma, but was surprised by the bitter sweet taste that greeted his taste buds. The blend of the two created a satisfying drink.

"That's quite good," Thorn said with a smile.

"Have you just arrived?"

"Yes."

"Is there anything I can help you with? Accommodation, entertainment?"

"No. I have somewhere to stay, thanks. I am looking for someone, though. You may be able to help. I understand he frequents this Station. His name is Ifor, another Earther like me."

There was a blank look on the Pertruans purple face. The marks on his cheeks seemed to spin or glow.

"No, I don't recall another Earther being in here. We don't get many of your kind on this Station so I would remember if there was one. Your best bet is to check with the Station master. He would know if there have been any other Earthers around."

"Thanks. I'll do that."

This had crossed Thorn's mind already, but since talking to the Station Master, he had sensed distrust in him. Besides, he felt that he knew what he was here for already. For now Thorn wanted to get his face known and show that he was serious in securing Ifor's services.

He finished his drink and left. The small device, no bigger than a flea, that had been following him since he left the Station Master dropped from the shadows and followed.

Thorn, Saul and Tianu all met after the two hours, each coming with the same information. Nothing. Thorn was not surprised. He expected at least a month of searching before any sort of contact.

The shuttle down to the surface took only ten minutes. Then another thirty minutes to their accommodation. The city was vast. The boundaries could just be made out as the shuttle entered the planet's atmosphere. It was equal in size to a continent on Earth; it sprawled across the surface like pond weed on water.

The landing area was circled by four vast towers that were the entrances to the four quarters of the south side of the city. All off-worlders tended to congregate there so Thorn thought this was the best place to stay and search for Ifor.

Their building contained six apartments spread over three floors. Thorn had reserved an apartment on the second floor. It housed three bedrooms, a lounging area and a balcony overlooking the hustle a bustle of the night life that entertained visitors. Though the area was busy, any noise that would have disturbed them was disbursed silently by the invisible field that covered the walkways.

"You two settle in here while I scout around outside. Study the maps of the area and plan out routes for us to take. We'll continue our search tomorrow. I'll bring back some food and clothes for you."

CHAPTER TWENTY

The days turned to weeks with no successful contact. They moved on to the next city. A completely different environment. Where the weather in Chaulk was warm and dry, Kriln was snow covered and cold. Still a very bright city from the sun in the sky, but the environment was a contrast to that of Chaulk. Each of the cities had their own micro climates that the Jornaerns could control. Something that had been successful for the last five hundred years.

The weeks turned into a month. Saul had given his communicator to a possible contact, but that had turned out to be a hoax. Thorn had been updated by Torst, but nothing much that aided them any further. The third city, Geesh, was underground. This was at the Northern most tip of the planet and here the environment couldn't be controlled. It was a harsh and barren place on the surface, so the Jornaerns created an underworld that was as fulfilling as any of the other cities. Great carvings had been created from the rocks and the city attracted artistic crowds that spent most of their time letting their creativity run wild.

Six weeks had now passed and the three of them were becoming weary and disillusioned. Thorn was beginning to question the reliability of Torst's information. How long should he continue before he decided that Ifor wasn't actually on this planet? Enyar would be back in a few weeks. Would he wait until they had finished? Thorn got the feeling that he wouldn't. He decided to consult with Torst again.

Later that evening he made contact. He explained his concerns about the information he was getting.

'I've had no indication that he's even been here let alone is here. I'd have thought someone would have at least heard of him'

'The information we are getting is very reliable. You must continue with your search. It is very important for the future, not of just my race, but of your own people.'

There was a moment's silence.

'There may be something that you can do to verify that he is on the planet. I'm not sure how effective it will be on such a large scale. I don't even know if you have the mental power. We've only been able to do it in a small city at best. That was only one of our kind. The majority of us can only perform it in a room.'

'What is it?'

'If you concentrate hard enough you may be able to spread your mind out across the city and sense if your friend is there.'

'Why didn't you tell me this before?'

'The stress could be too much for you. The one who managed to sense across the city ended up with irreparable brain damage. Even those of us who have

tried it in a room were incapacitated for a while. The potential for damage is enormous. I didn't want to chance it.'

'Well I'm going to try. If there is any way I can verify that he is here I'm willing to give it a go.'

'Whatever you do, don't perform it on your own. You need someone around you who could snap you out of it if they think it's going too far.'

'OK, I'll get Saul and Tianu to watch over me.'

Torst went on to explain the techniques to get Thorn's mind prepared for the mind spreading. He would have preferred to have been by Thorn's side at the time, but that was impossible. For now he had to trust in Saul and Tianu.

Thorn gathered the two together in the lounging area and explained what was going to happen.

"I need you to watch over me while I do this. I've no idea how it's going to affect me. If you think there's going to be a problem pull me back through the communicator."

Saul nodded as he rolled the communicator in his hand.

Thorn sat comfortably on a chair near the centre of the room. He closed his eyes, took a deep breath, relaxed and let his mind go. At first he was contained within the room, feeling as though there was a barrier preventing him from leaving. He looked at his body with the two young men looking on. He could see there was still a little tension in his body. Another deep breath and he was free. Out of the room, out of the building, sensing every life form as a dull outline close by.

Faster and faster his mind washed over the surrounding streets and buildings picking up every life sign there was. He slowed his progression to register the forms. Most he didn't recognise. The ones he had met over the time that they had been on Jornaer showed up as brighter shapes. Not of the being he knew. Just an irregular shape with no discernible form, but he could see with his mind's eye who it was.

The drunk on the shuttle to the bar area, the street speaker who was preaching, the numerous bar tenders and clientèle he had spoken to. All as clear to him as if they were in the same room. Further and further his mind went. The brighter forms were becoming less now. He was reaching the edges of the city and felt the blank coldness of the wasteland.

Back in the room, sweat trickled down the side of his head. Saul felt his forehead. He was getting hot. Saul left the room and returned with a cold wrap from the medi-kit that was attached to the wall in his bedroom and applied it to Thorn's head.

Across the wasteland and the mental wave grew larger and faster, ever increasing in speed. The next city and Thorn was having trouble recognising the brighter lights. They were still bright, but he couldn't pin point who they were exactly. Further and further onto more wasteland. Another city, more bright lights. The wave was almost uncontrollable. Still further it went, by now having covered half the planet.

Thorn's body began to tremble slightly. The sweat was making his skin shine.
"I think we should bring him back," said Tianu.
"Not yet. He's still got time."

Faster and faster he went tenuously hanging on. He felt as though he was on a ride and was slowly losing control. Still more bright lights and it was getting harder and harder to see their form. Now it was just a feeling of knowing them. That feeling you get when you see someone that sparks a light of recognition, but no matter how hard you try you can't find who they are in your mind. Faster, faster, another city, faster, faster, more wasteland, faster, faster...

CHAPTER TWENTY ONE

He didn't know what it was. A feeling? It was as though something had brushed his mind. Whatever it was it unnerved him and since being woken from his sleep he was unable to return.

He padded up and down the room unable to shake it off. He got himself a cold drink and eventually settled down to watch the entertainment viewer, the unease always with him.

Saul and Tianu watched on as the physician checked over Thorn. Since Saul had brought Thorn back he had been in an unconscious state. Tianu had found the Doctor at the local medical centre and persuaded him to come with the lure of credits.

"Physically he is fine. However, his mind is a different matter. It's like it has been wiped clean. There's no activity there at all." He turned to Tianu. "You say he had a fit. Well I'm afraid he's not going to recover. He will be in this state for the remainder of his life."

The two young men looked at the Jornaern shocked.

"I will leave my assistant here to look after your friend and return in a day. I will bring back some information on how you can proceed from here." He collected his things and left as the synthetic assistant took over.

A solemn silence fell over the room and hung there for what seemed like an eternity. The assistant busied itself around Thorn for a moment then stood next to him with the monitoring machine plugged into it and powered down to monitoring mode.

'Saul, Tianu...'

A recognisable, but weak voice came through to their minds.

'Thorn, is that you?' Saul replied.

'Yes...I'm very weak...but still alive. I need to shut down my brain for a while...Need time to repair...Stay close.' Then silence.

Both men turned to each other smiling.

"Don't worry. We're not going anywhere," said Tianu.

The next few days were spent by Thorn's side. The Doctor returned with information for the two men on what could be done for Thorn. Showing all of the procedures that could be performed to give him some sort of life. To keep the Doctor away, Tianu explained that they hadn't thought about what to do yet and would contact him when they had. To keep his assistant, a few more credits were added to the Doctors account.

Thorn would check in occasionally to let them know he was still around. Each time he would sound stronger. Saul and Tianu took it in turn to look over him while the other continued the search. Each time one of them went out, a familiar flea sized device would follow.

Day three and Saul and Tianu had just finished their morning meal. The rain had freshened the air and now the sun was drying the ground, a familiar sight in Taron, the city they now found themselves in. Tianu had settled down in a chair next to Thorn about to study and plan the routes for the next city. Saul was preparing to go into the market square that was the hub of this part of the city. The bars weren't as busy during the day, but the market square was and so were the eateries.

The sun shone through the window highlighting Thorn's hand that lay on his chest. A sudden flick of his finger cast a temporary shadow on his chest. Then another. Tianu looked up suddenly and caught the movement. He put down the Holo-Map and moved closer. The hand began to flex and Thorn's eyes slowly opened. Saul saw Tianu's movements as he came into the room.

"What is it?" He then saw the open eyes.

"Are you back?" asked Tianu.

Thorn turned his head towards the young man.

"I am and I'm very thirsty."

Fetching some water from the dispenser, Saul gave it to Thorn when he finally settled himself in to a sitting position. He drained the cup in a fraction of a second.

"How are you?" asked Saul.

"Still a little groggy and very hungry." He turned to the assistant. "They give you just enough to keep you alive."

"Was it successful?" said Tianu.

Thorn smiled.

"I sensed something, very slightly, that I'm convinced was Ifor. It was in the city of Jarad. That is where we must go next."

Jarad was situated towards the southern edge of Jornaer. A city grown from within a jungle. All of the living quarters and shops and bars were built from the wood of the Bangoi tree. The tree canopy above let in speckled light from the bright sun that shone almost all day allowing only a couple of hours of darkness.

In one part of the city a large residence sat entrenched in the thicker part of the jungle. An inconspicuous building indiscernible from many others close by. Inside Ifor was finishing off his breakfast of eggs and meat produced from the local animals. The experience of the previous night was wearing off slowly and he was beginning to feel like himself again.

He again began to think about the three men that were looking for him. Things had become quite hairy recently. Three jobs ago things hadn't quite gone to plan and since then he'd heard rumours that his then employers were looking for him. Bounty hunters had been sent to find him and he'd had to dispose of one of them already. From the description of the leader of this little group, it looked like another one had taken his place.

He flicked on the communicator button with his mind and a reply came back almost immediately.

"Yes boss?"

"Get four or five men together and send a welcoming party for the bounty hunter and his two friends. They should be turning up in a day or two. Use your best judgement as to how you deal with them. Remember, they could still be customers."

"Will do." The communicator fell silent and Ifor drained the last of his orange juice.

CHAPTER TWENTY TWO

The shuttle touched down just outside of the jungle area. The transport system branched off from here to all areas of the city. Thorn had already secured somewhere to stay and the three of them headed straight there.

Once again it was in the busy part of the city. It overlooked the bars in the centre of the city that was the best place to try to make contact with Ifor. There were a couple of hours before dark so they could have a scout around before it got too busy.

"I've marked out the best places to try on these maps," Saul said as he sent the Holo-Maps to the small devices Thorn and Tianu used during their searches. The three had discarded their gear in their rooms and were looking out over the area from their main balcony. The brightness of the sun was diluted and they could get away with just wearing normal sunglasses now. Rows upon rows of walkways weaved their way through the trees taking the walker to numerous bars and eateries. Though this city catered for a simpler way of life, technology was still employed in certain areas such as the sound diffusers that surrounded the bars and the fields that walled the walkways.

The walkways and ground covering below were made from a type of dark quartz that glistened from the speckled sunlight streaming through the canopy above and enthralled onlookers with its many colours. Tree trunks jutted out from every nook and cranny, or so it seemed, but the city and the jungle seemed to nestle neatly together.

"Let's get something to eat before we carry on with our search. The fresh food here has quite a reputation from what I've heard."

Saul and Tianu both nodded and followed Thorn out onto the walkways between the trees. The fresh breeze rustled the leaves and the scent that hung in the air teased out memories deep within Thorn's mind of Prius 3 and the lush vegetation that grew there. Memories that he hadn't visited for a long while.

The fresh food was indeed special. An array of fruits and succulent meats in locally made sauces played with their taste buds as they ate. Saul and Tianu had never had such delicacies before. So juicy, and soft and the flavours were to die for.

It was an hour before they resumed their search. They split up. Thorn took the bars at ground level. They were beginning to fill up slowly. In each one, wherever he went, the stares followed him. There can't have been many humans around here, if any. Or maybe they knew something he didn't. Either way he was getting the same old answers.

'Help, Thorn!'

The psychic cry came from Saul. Then the same from

Tianu. Then silence. He reached out with his mind to find them, still a little weak from his previous exertions. Once he found his bearings he set off.

"Going somewhere in a hurry are we?" came a voice ahead of him and he stopped abruptly before he could get in to his stride. In front of him stood two Jornaerns. Strong and muscular, they towered over him wearing what seemed like some sort of battle dress. Black leather like material had been turned into a vest and at the shoulders some sort of light armour covering. The black material continued onto their legs forming a one piece outfit. Shin high boots finished the look.

Thorn saw with his mind three more behind him. He quickly looked into the mind of the Jornaern who spoke and saw what had happened to Saul and Tianu. They were safe, just out of action for a while. This put him at ease.

"Who are you?" he asked.

"That's not your concern. What is your concern is how quickly you and your friends can leave this system."

The three Jornaerns moved a little closer to Thorn.

"I can't do that just yet. I'm looking for someone."

"That someone you are looking for isn't here, doesn't want to be found, is dead. Take your pick."

Thorn smiled knowing he had finally found his lead.

"Now I know the first and last part of that statement is untrue otherwise you wouldn't be here with your four friends."

The Jornaerns face changed as he realised that Thorn knew about his three colleagues behind him. He seemed a little flustered as he replied.

"Well...that doesn't matter as we're here to make sure you leave. The easy way or the hard way."

Thorn tried to reason with him.

"I just want to see him for a short while. Tell him I'm an old friend from way back."

It didn't work. The Jornaern pulled out a laser whip from his belt that cracked the air as it flailed around. The other four followed suit. The hum in the air was kind of soothing in a deadly way and it massaged Thorn's mind for a split second distracting him. It was almost costly. As the first whip hit him his coat deflected it harmlessly out of the way. Then four more hits knocked him to the ground. One whip caught him on the cheek and it opened a two inch cut, knocking his sunglasses to the floor.

He let out a yelp of pain and cupped his cheek with his hand. He was temporarily blinded by the sudden bright light on his eyes, but closed them instantly and his mind took over. A temporary field enveloped his body deflecting the blows from the whips. This proved to be more exhausting than Thorn first thought.

He had to think quickly. Catching his sunglasses with his mind he threw them through the air at such a speed that when it hit the lead Jornaern it broke his nose. The whip dropped from his hand and he fell backwards to the ground. There was a split second when everyone stopped. This was Thorn's chance. He dropped the field around him, relieving the stress on his mind and jumped over to the fallen whip grabbing it as he forward rolled.

The four standing Jornaerns regained composure and readjusted their distance to Thorn to continue their assault. Thorn grabbed the closest with his mind and dragged him forwards so that he would take the full force of the next onslaught. Which he did to his fellow comrade's dismay. The three weapons left their vicious marks on his body, shredding clothing and skin alike. The shrill cry from his lips lasted at least a minute while he lay on the floor writhing around in agony.

Thorn was now on his feet, whip dangling by his side. The three remaining Jornaerns, a male and two females hesitated on their next move.

"I don't want to hurt any more of you. I just want to speak to Ifor." Thorn tried the peaceful approach. Again it didn't work. The male pulled out a laser gun from behind his back and took aim. Immediately Thorn's mind took it from his grasp and broke it in half in mid air right in front of a startled face. He took the hint and fled into the narrow alleyways behind him. The two females didn't take long to follow.

Thorn dropped the whip and knelt down beside the lead Jornaern. Blood was pouring through his hands as they cupped his nose.

"I want you to take me to my companions," he said to the forlorn figure. A low rumbling growl emanated from the Jornaerns throat as he got to his feet.

Thorn was led through the small alleyways for about twenty minutes before coming upon a solid wooden door to a tall warehouse type building. The Jornaern banged on the door three times then paused and then banged another four times. Footsteps could be heard coming towards the door until it opened slightly and a scarred face peered through the gap. As soon as it did Thorn kicked the door open. The Jornaern behind it went skidding across the floor and was pinned down by a force he could not see.

"Which way now?" Thorn followed the Jornaern up a flight of stairs, passed some unused and trashed offices to a room at the far end of the corridor.

"You go in first," he whispered to the Jornaern.

The door opened to a large room that directly overlooked the empty warehouse space below. The five Jornaerns inside were a little surprised when they saw their leader with red blood smeared over his face. Then when they saw Thorn they jumped into action grabbing for the weapons that they had left lying around on the tables they had been sitting at.

Too late. Thorn had whipped the weapons into a pile in the corner.

"Stop! At ease. I don't think you will stand much chance against this human. Let him be."

The five Jornaerns took a step backwards in response to their leader. Thorn saw to the left side of the room Saul and Tianu were laying on the floor. He went over to them.

"They are not harmed. Just a mild plant sedative that will wear off in a couple of hours. We were only sent to meet up with you and warn you away. Things got a little...out of hand. No hard feelings I hope?"

Thorn took no notice of what was said as he examined the two lying on the floor. He looked back up to the leader and pulled out the communicator.

"Give this to Ifor and get him to contact me. We'll arrange a meet then."

CHAPTER TWENTY THREE

"What do you mean he's psychic? Is he a TechPsycher?"

Zorba was favouring his broken nose. He'd had a few broken noses in his time so it was an annoyance as much as anything else. He was trying to explain to Ifor of the encounter.

"He didn't have a headband, but he is definitely from Earth."

"Then they must have come up with some other way of giving them the psychic powers. A new breed of TechPsycher. God knows what they've done to these people to get them to this point."

"Whatever it is he is very powerful. Maybe more so than you."

Ifor shot Zorba a sharp look.

"Then we should go prepared with the element of surprise. Pelios!" he shouted to the next room.

A moment later a six foot human walked into the room. The same build and skin tone as Ifor, but some fifty years younger. He threw the communicator to the advancing man.

"I want you to contact this man pretending to be me and arrange a meet in the wasteland just outside the southern gate. About a mile outside by the abandoned camp. Make it for night fall where we'll have more cover. Zorba, round up five or six bodies and one good marksman. Place him on the large rock just outside the camp. Let's find out what this bum wants."

As Thorn made his way to the meeting point the night descended quickly. The three moons cast multiple shadows on the ravaged ground. Saul and Tianu had stayed back in the city under his instructions. Although he hadn't seen Ifor for over thirty years there was something about the message he had received about the meet that didn't sound like him. It made him suspicious. If there was to be any trouble he didn't want to have to worry about them. There may yet still be a trap waiting.

The camp, one of many dotted around the city circumference, lay in a ruinous state. Once home to many activities that were outlawed in the city, it was left empty when the city law enforcers actually did something about it. They thought the camps couldn't survive out here in the wasteland with the violent weather changes and wild creatures. But they underestimated the resilience and fortitude of the locals and finally gathered a strike force that took out the camps in one fell swoop. The violent and bloody fight was a black mark on Jarads history.

As expected, there were eight figures waiting for Thorn when he got there. A large fire had been started to combat the low temperatures once the sun had set. The figures had their backs to the fire as they watched Thorn walk up to them.

"Who is this human who seeks an audience with me," bellowed Pelios slightly overplaying his role.

Thorn stopped twenty paces from him. He could not see Pelios's face, but he knew from the sound of the voice it wasn't Ifor.

"I don't know who you are, but I've come here to speak with Ifor."

"I am Ifor!" Pelios tried and failed to sound convincing.

As Thorn scanned the other figures he could just about make out that each one was wearing the armour of the Jornaerns he had encountered earlier in the day, but they also wore masks that covered the top half of their faces.

"Enough of this charade. Show your face like the man you are supposed to be." With that Thorn ripped off every single mask and pointed at Ifor. "You are the one I have come to see!" When Thorn saw Ifor's face for the first time in over thirty years, emotions began to swirl around his mind. So much so that if the Jornaerns had decided to attack at that moment he would have been defenceless.

Ifor stepped forward in front of Pelios.

"Who are you?"

Thorn fought back the emotion to speak.

"Has it been so long that you do not recognise me, my brother?"

Ifor moved a little closer getting a better look at the face using the light from the fire. A spark of recognition softened his features and his eyes slowly widened.

"Thorn? Is that you?"

Thorn nodded.

"My God, Thorn!" Ifor rushed over to him and they both hugged and jumped around like two schoolboys who had just told each other that they had lost their virginity.

CHAPTER TWENTY FOUR

The two men spoke for hours back at Ifor's house. Ifor regaled Thorn with tales of his mercenary life and some of the close shaves he had. The rum flowed freely long into the next day.

"I never pictured you in this kind of environment," Thorn gestured out of the glassless window to the thick woods beyond.

"It's the only place on this whole planet that I don't need my eye protectors. Besides, I need the peace every now and then."

Thorn fell silent for a moment.

"The others are still alive. Just like you they don't know of each other's existence. We have to get back together again and continue the fight against the TechPsychers. We can end their domination once and for all."

The constant smile that had been on Ifor's face since he had recognised Thorn slowly disappeared.

"I don't know, Thorn. They've gotten a hell of a lot

more powerful in the time we've been out of action. They've pretty much sewn up the whole galaxy. There's only a few planets they haven't reached yet and it won't be much longer before they've got them in their control. Besides, I've got a nice little life here now."

Anger erupted in Thorn like a volcano.

"And what about all of those millions of innocent Naturals that are being hunted down and experimented on. Have they got a nice little life? Do they have big houses to go home to without fear of being invaded and dragged away to god knows where?" He leaned on the window sill and gripped it, turning his knuckles white, hoping to control his anger. "Time has changed you, Ifor. Somehow your morals have been corrupted. Selfless help for the needy has become selfish and needy." Thorn turned to Ifor and glared at him. "I hope you never experience what our home world Naturals experience." Thorn left before he said something he would regret.

Ifor gripped his glass. He reached out with his mind and threw a chair across the room smashing it and part of the wooden wall it hit.

Thorn had slept for ten hours before waking to the darkness again. Disappointment still choked his heart. He rose from his bed and headed straight for the shower. Not even the coldness of the water could change his mood.

In the main living area, Tianu was still awake watching some local entertainment on the wall viewer. He turned around as Thorn came into the room.

"How was your reunion? Have you managed to sleep off the after effects?"

Thorn requested cold water from the dispenser.

"As soon as you and Saul have rested for the night we'll head back to Chaulk. Enyar should be back in a week or so."

Tianu looked a little confused.

"What about Ifor?"

The cold water burned the back of Thorn's throat.

"Looks like he won't be joining us."

"Why? What happened?"

"He's been away from the fight for too long. Seems like the mercenary lifestyle has diluted his morals. I was expecting...more."

A banging on the door broke into the conversation.

"Who's around at this time of night," said Thorn. He released his mind to wander outside of the building to find Ifor at the door. A look of surprise tightened the skin around his eyes. Tianu got up to open the door.

"Is he in?" Ifor asked.

"Yes." Tianu stepped aside as Ifor walked past and stopped in front of Thorn.

"You're right! I've let it go for too long. I can't stand by any longer. My exile to this side of the galaxy has clouded my...our real purpose in life. We were born to free our people, no matter the odds."

A smile crept over Thorn's face.

"I think the odds have swung in our favour, my friend. Have you noticed a change in your psychic abilities since that trap on earth?"

Ifor nodded.

"Yes, I have. And they have improved significantly over the years."

"I'm betting the same has happened to the others. I've been honing my abilities for the last thirty years with the help of an alien from Vulzeon. His race has a long story that involves the TechPsychers, but that's for another day. Before the psychic bomb took us out, these aliens were monitoring us and by their calculations, if each one of us has had changes to our mind as I have, with the right nurturing, we could be powerful enough to take down the TechPsychers once and for all."

Ifor beamed at that thought. It disappeared almost immediately. "I have one more job I need to do before I can go anywhere, though. It should only take a day or so. It's one I can't leave. It's for a very influential individual and I don't want to be upsetting her. Why don't you come along and I'll introduce you to my baby."

Thorn looked puzzled.

"OK. Why not?"

CHAPTER TWENTY FIVE

Six hours later Ifor and Thorn were standing next to a Star fighter.

"Meet my baby," said Ifor. "She's still young, relatively speaking, but boy can she move. I don't know of a single craft that can out manoeuvre her or catch her when she's in full flight. Come on in." Ifor bounded up the ramp like a lamb in the spring with Thorn following on behind.

It had been a long time since he had been in a Star fighter. The closeness of the walls brought back memories of the Savage Mind all those years earlier. The sounds, the smells. All so familiar, as was the outline of the ship when they approached.

The long corridor led to a ladder which in turn led up to another corridor which took the two men into the heart of the fighter. The control centre. Once again a familiarity gripped Thorn.

"Do you recognise anything yet?" Ifor asked looking at Thorn.

"It does have a familiar feel about it."

"I had it built to my own specs. I tried a lot of ships, but never felt quite at home with them. So I had this built. It's modelled on the Savage Mind. With all new technology, of course, and a few alterations compared to a regular fighter to accommodate my new abilities."

Thorn looked around the room. It was spacious compared to anything he had seen in the ship so far. Towards the front of the room was a large display area covering the wall. In the centre of the room a main chair sat with six more arranged around it. Ifor flopped down in the main chair.

"Take a seat. Lift off is usually a bumpy affair on this planet."

The fighter rose from the landing site with an elegant lift, nosing gently skywards. It was out of the Jornaern atmosphere within a minute and hitting its maximum speed thirty seconds later heading for the Cold Region, a desolate and isolated area of the Helix System. The Cold Region contained nothing that would be classified as a planet. However, large rocks, with the biggest being half the size of Jornaer, circled what seemed to be nothingness. That is nothingness that could be explained. A perfect circle had been followed, for as long as there had been anyone in the System, by the rocks, but no one could explain what they were circling.

Nothing had ever been detected in the area that would be of any use to anyone so it had never been visited. Until eight years ago.

A wealthy family from the planet Ion in the Gamma System had begun mining the rocks. Nobody knew what for. The Ioneons had brought their own labour, never needing to hire from the local planets, so no information was ever found out about what was going on in that area. Until Ifor's employer, being the business woman she was, discovered the secret.

"That's when she sought me out. She claimed it was a job only I could do and if the Ioneons knew of my existence they would try to force me to work for them. It seems there is some relic from, get this, another Dimension, which is buried deep in one of those rocks."

"You seem very sceptical! I take it you completely dismiss the idea of Dimensions beyond our own!"

Ifor sat up straight.

"Until now I thought we all did. What's changed your opinion?"

"Let's just say I've experienced things that make me more open to the idea."

"Awww, come on Thorn! We live in the real world. We don't take any notice of every Occultist we meet. What is...is! What we touch, what we feel through our minds. That experience is all there is."

Thorn paused before replying.

"Maybe." He steered the direction of the conversation. "What is it that only you can do on this rock?"

"It seems the relic is held in some kind of field. Nothing can penetrate it. Nothing, that is except a psycher. The Ioneons have had limited success with some TechPsychers that they've managed to employ, but it's still there. And by all accounts they're off tracking down more TechPsychers to continue the work. There should be limited resistance when we get there."

Thorn frowned.

"What do you mean by limited resistance?"

"The last report we had said there were just a handful

of guards. Nothing for us to worry about."

Thorn sank back in his chair. Ifor was facing him from the main chair and saw his unease.

"Come on. There's nothing to worry about. Just sit back and enjoy the ride. We should be there in four hours."

CHAPTER TWENTY SIX

The fighter, which Ifor had also named The Savage Mind, glided into the Cold Region and proceeded to the largest rock in orbit. A probe had been sent on ahead of them checking for mines within the region, carefully mapping a safe route. To Ifor's surprise no traps were found. The path through was as smooth as a ride on a giant sloth.

The Savage Mind held back from landing until the probe had searched the mined area of the rock for the remaining guards. The report back was unexpected.

"Nothing!" Ifor said with raised eyebrows. "Not a single guard. No life signs whatsoever."

"Would they have abandoned the place?" asked Thorn.

Ifor shook his head.

"From what I understand the relic is invaluable."

"Are you sure the relic is still there?"

Ifor moved the probe deeper into the mine shaft with his mind. Fifteen minutes later it was in a large cavern where at the centre stood an alter that was carved out of the very rock itself. On the alter stood a triangular shaped object. It gently glowed in an unseen light.

"It doesn't look much, but I'd say that is what we're looking for."

The scene hovered over the table as a 3D holographic image.

"I don't like it, Ifor! Something's wrong! I'm going to have a look around."

Thorn closed his eyes and let his mind go. Out of the space craft and across the void between fighter and rock. He covered as much as he could, conscious of his weakened mind. Nothing! In the cavern and shafts leading to it. A half mile radius around the mining site. All as cold and empty as the space around them.

Sweat was beginning to appear on Thorn's forehead now. He took a moment to compose himself.

"I can't find anything."

"Then we go in," said Ifor.

The Savage Mind's auto pilot took the craft to a landing point three hundred yards from the shaft entrance. Its landing lights illuminated the temporary buildings set out in a semi circle to the right of the entrance. As the ramp came down, eight of Ifor's team followed Zorba out, laser guns at the ready. Each took a point around the ship scanning the surrounding area. Ifor and Thorn followed on behind.

The temperature was below zero and everyone dressed in thermal clothing with a thermal balaclava type hood wrapped around their heads. Thorn had his long jacket on top of this. There was no ice on the rock face. No water droplets had ever existed in the Cold Region.

"Zorba, take four and check out the buildings. The

rest of you come with me." Frozen breath billowed out as he spoke. It was then he noticed how silent it was. A silence he had never experienced before. It unnerved him almost to the point of turning round and flying away. He shook his head and carried on.

The six of them reached the shaft entrance in a semi circle twenty paces apart.

It wasn't a large shaft. In fact it looked just like a regular passageway with a very high ceiling. Lamps were evenly spaced along the shaft on either side giving off enough light for Ifor to see where he walked negating the need for the torch he carried.

He took the lead with Thorn close behind him. They worked their way slowly down the shaft. Five minutes in and they came to an unlit area. The lights ahead showed where the shaft continued. Ifor flicked the torch back on to reveal a domed room big enough to fit the Savage Mind in. The wall surfaces were smooth just like the main shaft walls. But here there were insignias and what looked like religious markings covering every inch of their surface.

As the piercing beam scanned the room it caught something glistening to the left on the far side. Ifor slowly made his way over keeping the light on it. A sickening stench immediately met him and he cupped his free hand to his mouth and nose. As he moved forward the floor became sticky. He shone the light down. A bright red substance covered the floor in pools. Shining the torch back up he could now see what was hidden in the dark. He counted four mangled skeletons with strips of rotting flesh and muscle still hanging from their bones.

"What the hell's happened here!" he spluttered.

Thorn joined him, also with his mouth and nose covered. He manoeuvred his torch around the rest of the room and found piles of bones littering the floor. Bending down he picked one up to examine it.

"Do you think this is some sort of sacrificial room?" asked Ifor.

"I don't know, but these bones have teeth marks on them." He showed Ifor the indentations.

"Big teeth as well by the looks of it. But we didn't pick up any life signs! And some of these look pretty fresh." Ifor activated his communicator. "Zorba. We may have company. Keep on your toes. Our sensors seem to be useless here so you're going to have to rely on your eyes."

"Will do," came the reply.

The group carried on through the shaft until they eventually reached the main cavern. It was huge, but there wasn't a part of it that was in darkness. There was no need for lamps in here because light bounced off of every surface. It was hard to determine where the source was. The walls and floor were just rock, the same rock they had seen in the shafts. There was no glow from the relic itself. The light was just...there.

Ifor's team walked the perimeter of the cavern while he and Thorn approached the relic. His communicator sparked into life piercing through the silence.

"We've found nothing out here. What do you want us to do?"

"Leave two guarding the entrance to the shaft and the rest of you come and join us," Ifor replied.

"OK." The silence returned.

The two men were ten steps from the relic when they felt a force push against them. Only lightly at first until they were six steps away and then they felt they were up against a brick wall. The pressure on their bodies forced them back.

"Step back a minute," said Ifor. He raised his gun and fired. The green bolt of light disappeared, swallowed by the force field. "Wow! Neat," he smiled. "These Ioneon's have got some cool technology."

Thorn shook his head.

"Not sure it's their technology. I can't see a power source. Maybe it's natural. It must be the reason you were chosen for the job. See if you can reach in with your mind."

Ifor lowered his weapon and concentrated on the relic. He could feel the power as his mind closed in, squeezing it, but it wasn't stopping him. It was hard going and Ifor began to sweat. First salty water, then blood began to drip from his eyes. Thorn saw the trouble Ifor was in and immediately joined his mind. He too felt the power of the field. Squeezing and ripping at his mind. They reached and surrounded the relic lifting it from its resting place. The return was just as hard. Beads of blood were appearing on Thorn's forehead now.

Back up the shaft a bright light suddenly illuminated their bodies. Screams followed immediately and then a blood curdling roar, the like no one in the cavern had heard before. It lasted a good thirty seconds before the sound of crunching bones replaced it.

CHAPTER TWENTY SEVEN

Ifor and Thorn staggered back as the relic was finally released from its protective field and it dropped gently to the floor. More screams and Zorba came running from the shaft like a crazed animal.

"What is it?" Ifor asked in a weak and tired voice.

"The Krillar! The Krillar!"

Thorn turned to Ifor, confused.

"It's the Jornaern version of the devil," Ifor answered the unasked question.

Thorn didn't have time for any more questions as the Krillar came lolloping into the cavern, one of Ifor's teams limbs still hanging from the giants jaw. It stood a full fifteen feet high. Now Thorn knew why the shafts ceilings were so high. Another terrifying roar and the limb fell to the ground. The poor victim's blood dribbled down the monsters chin.

Scales covered the body that looked as hard as rock. The head, a little oversized for the body, was dominated by a massive mouth full of razor sharp teeth. Its deformed skull resembled an outcrop of rocks with two blood red eyes set on storks that protruded outwards a couple of inches. The long arms ended in talon like hands each with four digits that were mirrored on the end of its powerful legs. It looked around the cavern and its eyes came to rest on the relic.

Ifor shot a quick glance at Thorn.

"Any ideas?"

Before he could answer the Jornaerns opened fire sending a shower of laser bolts at the creature. Each one just bounced off of the scales and fizzed into the walls. This went on for a minute until they gave up.

"The weapons are having no effect!" shouted one of the shooters.

"Oh yes it is!" Ifor said. "It's making it angry."

Another shrill roar rang through the cavern bouncing off the walls as the monster strode forward towards the source of the laser bolts. It wasn't fast by any means, but its reach fooled the first two Jornaerns and they screamed as the blows from its talons ripped through their clothing and flesh leaving their innards exposed and free from containment. As the two dropped to the floor the gore and blood pooled around them.

The few moments since the monster appeared, Ifor and Thorn had made a small recovery from their ordeal with the relic and were frantically trying to come up with a plan.

"We should try and out run it," said Ifor. "It'll never catch us." He picked up the relic with a bit of an effort. "Wow, that's heavy." The smooth sides were like nothing he had felt before and even holding it by the base he had trouble trying to stop it from slipping from his hands. The Krillar saw this and lumbered towards the two men.

Zorba and the remaining two Jornaerns ran for the shaft. Halfway into it a brilliant light blinded them for a second. Then another roar, this time from within the shaft. Another Krillar was heading straight for them. The Jornaerns now became hysterical. They started blasting away at the monster in the shaft while backing away. A rain of laser bolts came back at them, bouncing off of the Krillars scales. Zorba died instantly. Two other injured bodies fell to the ground. The monster descended on them and caught their heads in its claws, squeezing until their skulls crushed and their brains oozed out and flopped to the floor.

Thorn and Ifor retreated further into the cavern. The second Krillar came in to view still feasting on one of the Jornaerns and with the crushed skulls still in it's grip.

"You're gonna have to give the relic back," Thorn said to Ifor. "They must be here to protect it."

"What!" A look of dismay crossed Ifor's face. "There must be another way!" Ifor racked his brains for another solution, but found nothing as the creatures came closer. Finally he sent the relic over with his mind. He laid it gently at the feet of the first Krillar.

Both of them raised their heads to the roof of the cavern and let out an almighty roar that shook the very ground they were standing on. Then continued their pursuit.

"So much for that idea. What now?" Ifor said backing further away.

"I'm going to try something." Thorn stood still and closed his eyes.

"What are you doing?"

Thorn reached out with his mind, searching. Deep

inside the first Krillar's mind he searched. Deeper and deeper. How primitive everything was. Full of rage. The swirling vortex that was the Krillar's mind unnerved him. Its violent and primitive feel was so...familiar. Thorn ploughed on through the turmoil until...There! That's what he was looking for.

By now the two monsters were almost an arm's length away. The first Krillar swung back ready to strike, talons outstretched, ready to rip apart whatever it came into contact with.

"Thorn!" Ifor shouted, urging him to move. The taloned arm swept round just over the head of Thorn and ripped an eye from the stalk of the second Krillar. It turned to face its new foe and let loose with a barrage of blows that tore scales from the body and ripped long gashes in the exposed flesh. The fighting was fierce and primal. The second Krillar was stunned at first, but fought back just as viciously even with one eye missing. At first they fought in the way of the exit and Thorn and Ifor were still trapped. But soon they were stumbling around the cavern, baring their teeth and roaring a cry that shook the walls.

Both men took their chance with Ifor grabbing the relic on the way. They ran as fast as their legs would take them. Very soon they were running out of breath, realising how much the retrieval of the relic had taken out of them physically. They were now stumbling to the entrance of the shaft and they could just about see the Savage Mind. Ifor sent ahead the commands to get the ship set for take-off. There was no sign of the two Jornaerns left to guard the entrance. Ifor reached out with his mind, but found no one else around.

Thorn concentrated on the sounds coming from the

cavern. He could hear only a single roar now. And it was heading their way.

"It's coming after us!" he shouted.

The adrenalin rushed round their bodies giving them an extra kick. They were soon clambering up the ramp and into the ship. As it took off the back jolted a little.

"What was that?" asked Ifor. He scanned the exterior of the ship.

"The damn thing won't give up," he said. "Strap yourself in. It's going to be a rough ride."

Both men secured themselves into their chairs. The three crew members that had remained on the ship were already seated. With Ifor now in full control of the Savage Mind he immediately flipped it upside down. The creatures talons had dug deep into the outer skin and it hung there with its legs flailing until a fast approaching outcrop of rock smashed it from its holding point crushing its bones and internal organs. The Savage Mind flipped back upright and escaped the Cold Region as fast as it could, heading for Jornaer.

CHAPTER TWENTY EIGHT

"What was that thing and where did it come from? We found no signs of life down there. It's as if it just magically appeared from nowhere." Ifor was wiping his face and forehead of the blood that had stained there while a Medibot was checking him over. Thorn sat with the relic on his knees and stared at the smooth surfaces, entranced. He wasn't aware of Ifor's words. It was like his mind was being massaged by the aura from the relic, shutting out everything around him.

The jolt was sudden as Ifor took the relic and dumped it on another chair.

"Are you listening to me?" he said.

Thorn shook his head to clear it from the drowsy feeling he now experienced.

"I...I missed it. What did you say again?"

"What do you mean you missed it? What's the matter? You seem...distracted."

"I don't know. There's something about that thing. Don't you feel anything from it?"

"All I can feel now is a headache when I look at it. The sooner we get rid of it the better."

"I wonder what it's for. I've seen some scary things in my time, but nothing like those two... creatures. What were they? Whatever they were the relic must be very precious to someone. What have you got yourself mixed up in, Ifor?"

Ifor had settled back down for the Medibot to continue its work.

"It's just a job. Once we've delivered it we'll be gone and won't have to worry about it."

Thorn sensed Ifor was getting annoyed. There was a short silence before Thorn continued.

"Where do you think they appeared from?" Thorn stared into Ifor's eyes. Ifor shifted uncomfortably as he thought about the creatures and shrugged his shoulders.

"My guess would be that they're creatures from the Jornaerns past. Something that hasn't been seen in thousands of years and have embedded themselves in the local myths and beliefs. Perhaps they have a way of hiding themselves that our detectors can't pick up."

"Perhaps! But what about the light before they appeared? What do you think that was?"

"I don't know. Maybe it was their white teeth when they smiled that lit up the shaft. I don't particularly care. Let's just get rid of the damn thing and go find the other guys."

The rest of the journey was a chance to recover fully from the ordeal on the lump of rock that imprisoned the relic. The relic itself was stowed away securely, but every time Thorn walked by it, a drawing power pulled on his mind. The first time it happened he almost gave in to the unseen force. He almost opened up the container and took out the relic to touch its smooth sides again. But he resisted and pulled himself away from the storage area. On three more occasions he had to pass it and each time the draw became less.

The Savage Mind made its final approach to Jornaer a day and a half later. It was heading for the North of the planet to the city of Jorn, the very first city of the modern era to be completed. Technology was its attraction. Everything was geared around pleasure and the service of the inhabitants. If they didn't want to, the Jornaerns didn't have to move a muscle to get from one place to the next. They could be transported from one side of the city to the other without moving a limb. They just had to think it and the mechanical Personal Aid that each Jornaern had would move them.

The whole city was connected through a series of neural links that in turn connected to each PA. The Jornaerns had to just link up and they could be anywhere they wanted to be and do anything they wanted to do. There was only a small percentage of Jornaerns that would stay in this city for long periods. Some had been there for most of their lives and their bodies were in no condition to be able to withstand the effort of moving unaided. Generally it was a city for a break.

Ifor's employer had arranged to take possession of the relic here. She was based on the east side and as the Savage Mind came in to land, an uneasy feely grew within the two men.

"Something's not quite right," Thorn said. "We've had no request for clearance codes."

The Savage Mind gently settled on the landing pad. Here was a secluded area that had a hang up from the first settlers. A wealthy area that distinguished itself from any other place on Jornaer by being available only to those that were deemed to be worthy. A self appointed committee would determine the fate of any prospective tenant.

This area of the city was secluded from the rest. Set aside for the powerful and influential of Jornaer. It covered around ten acres and was the epitome of excess. Though the cities on Jornaer were equal in their wealth, because Jorn was the first, it suffered from a misguided feeling of self-importance. Exclusivity not only holidayed here, it was the law.

Thorn and Ifor alighted from the ship with Thorn carrying the relic in its container. The strange power that emanated from it was too much for Ifor and Thorn seemed to be more in control over its pull now. As a precaution both men were dressed in battle gear. Thorn in his long coat with gun holstered inside it. Ifor wore the Jornaern battle dress of shoulder, arm, chest and leg guards with his gun holstered to his right hand side.

They entered the greeting area where they expected to be met by a greeter. Nothing. It was quiet. Deathly quiet. Both men stopped at a Holo-Map that filled the far wall. Ifor studied it.

"There's something wrong. There's no sign of anyone here. This map should be bustling with the movement of everyone in this area. It just looks as though the place is empty."

Thorn reached out with his mind and confirmed what Ifor had said.

"Are you sure this was where you were supposed to meet?"

"As sure as I'm standing here. Something's very wrong." Ifor looked around the room. It was domed and rose to a height of thirty metres. He noticed something on one of the walls that ran up and along the domed ceiling. He took a closer look. Markings, just like the symbols on the rock they had escaped from not two days ago, meandered their way across the wall.

"Does this look familiar to you?"

Thorn looked and nodded.

"If what happened here is connected with the relic, we'd better keep an eye out for those creatures." He turned to Ifor. "Are you sure you don't know what that things for?"

"No, I swear! As far as I'm concerned it's just another religious piece of junk. Like so many they seem to treasure."

"Let's take a look around."

Both of them moved off cautiously. Occasionally Thorn would make a quick search ahead with his mind, never finding anyone or any more signs of the creatures. They came to a large set of doors that led into a meeting area for the inhabitants. It had been filled with trees and plants and gently burbling streams. Tranquillity captured for all that had now been devastated by a brutal, destructive force.

"What the hell happened here?" said Thorn. The resulting carnage was as though a hurricane had been let loose and amongst this destruction pools of blood covered fleshless Jornaern bones. No plant, no cobble had been left unturned.

"I think it's time we left," said Ifor.

"I make you right."

The End.

Thank you for reading my story. If you have the time please write an honest review to let other people know what you thought of it.

ABOUT P.B.THOMPSON

P.B.Thompson works full-time in IT and his spare time is divided between his writing and spending time with his partner and three young boys. His writing schedule is full with planned books in Fantasy, Crime, Mystery, Horror and continuing with the Psychic Knights series.